FUN學

美國英語閱讀課本

各學科實用課文 三版

3

U0033924

+ Workbook

AMERICAN SCHOOL TEXTBOOK

READING KEY

作者 Michael A. Putlack & e-Creative Contents　　譯者 鄭玉瑋

MP3
寂天雲 APP

如何下載 MP3 音檔

❶ 寂天雲 APP 聆聽：掃描書上 QR Code 下載「寂天雲－英日語學習隨身聽」APP。加入會員後，用 APP 內建掃描器再次掃描書上 QR Code，即可使用 APP 聆聽音檔。

❷ 官網下載音檔：請上「寂天閱讀網」（www.icosmos.com.tw），註冊會員／登入後，搜尋本書，進入本書頁面，點選「MP3 下載」下載音檔，存於電腦等其他播放器聆聽使用。

American School Textbook
Reading Key

The Best Preparation for Building Academic Reading Skills and Vocabulary

The Reading Key series is designed to help students to understand American school textbooks and to develop background knowledge in a wide variety of academic topics. This series also provides learners with the opportunity to enhance their reading comprehension skills and vocabulary, which will assist them when they take various English exams.

Reading Key <Volume 1-3> is
a three-book series designed for beginner to intermediate learners.

Reading Key <Volume 4-6> is
a three-book series designed for intermediate to high-intermediate learners.

Reading Key <Volume 7-9> is
a three-book series designed for high-intermediate learners.

Features

- A wide variety of topics that cover American school subjects
  helps learners expand their knowledge of academic topics through interdisciplinary studies

- Intensive practice for reading skill development
  helps learners prepare for various English exams

- Building vocabulary by school subjects and themed texts
  helps learners expand their vocabulary and reading skills in each subject

- Graphic organizers for each passage
  show the structure of the passage and help to build summary skills

- Captivating pictures and illustrations related to the topics
  help learners gain a broader understanding of the topics and key concepts

Table of Contents

Social Studies • History and Geography

Chapter 2 Science

Chapter 3
Mathematics • Language • Visual Arts • Music

Workbook for Daily Review

Syllabus Vol. 3

Subject	Topic & Area	Title
Social Studies ★ **History and Geography**	Technology	How Transportation Has Changed
	Technology	Inventors and Inventions
	Government	Choosing Our Leaders
	Government	Presidents' Day in February
	World Geography	Countries Have Neighbors
	World Geography	The Amazon Rain Forest
	World Geography	Protecting the Earth
	World Geography	The World's Endangered Animals
	Culture	World Religions
	Culture	Religious Holidays
	American History	Early Travelers to America
	American History	The Pilgrims and Thanksgiving
Science	Our Earth	Inside the Earth
	Our Earth	Earthquakes and Volcanoes
	The Solar System	Why Does the Moon Seem to Change?
	The Solar System	The First Man on the Moon
	Electricity and Energy	Electricity
	Electricity and Energy	Conserving Electricity
	Motion and Energy	Motion and Forces
	Motion and Energy	Magnets
	Sound	What Is Sound?
	Sound	Sounds and Safety
	The Human Body	The Organs of the Human Body
	The Human Body	The Five Senses
Mathematics	Numbers and Operations	Word Problems
	Numbers and Operations	Place Value
	Multiplication and Division	Multiplication and Division
	Multiplication and Division	Skip Counting Equal Groups
Language and Literature	Myths	What Are Myths?
	Myths	Prometheus Brings Fire
	Language Arts	Nouns
	Language Arts	Some Common Sayings
Visual Arts	Visual Arts	Realistic Art and Abstract Art
	Visual Arts	Picasso and His Work
Music	A World of Music	Many Kinds of Music
	A World of Music	Modern Music

1

- **Social Studies**
- **History and Geography**

How Transportation Has Changed

 01

New technology changes the way people live.

Technology is using science to make things faster or better.

Key Words

• technology

• transportation

• travel

• wagon

• nowadays

• subway

• airplane

• goods

• at one time

Let's learn how transportation has changed thanks to technology.

In the past, it took days to travel by horse and wagon.

Nowadays, people travel faster and easier in many ways.

We drive cars, trucks, and buses.

We ride on trains and subways.

We sail on ships and even fly on airplanes.

Many kinds of transportation are also used to carry goods.

A truck can carry goods all over the country.

A train can carry a lot of goods at one time.

An airplane and ship can take goods around the world.

Transportation moves people and goods from one place to another.

Thanks to new technology, transportation is changing quickly and safely.

✔ How Travel Has Changed

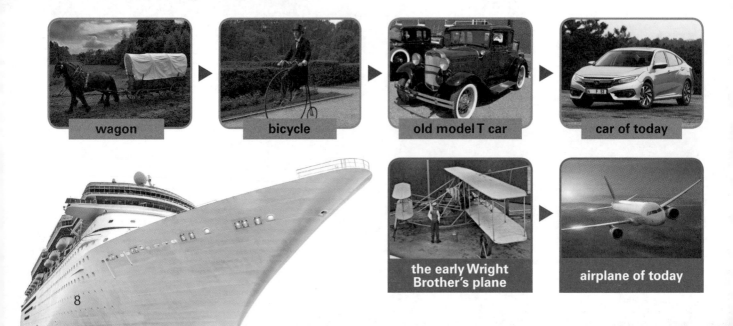

wagon ▶ bicycle ▶ old model T car ▶ car of today

the early Wright Brother's plane ▶ airplane of today

8

Main Idea and Details

1   What is the passage mainly about?

a. Transporting moves goods from one place to another.

b. It's the best way for people to travel nowadays.

c. Some ways traveling and transportation have changed.

2   People can _____ in the air on airplanes.

a. sail   b. fly   c. ride

3   Which method of transportation did people use in the past?

a. Airplanes.   b. Automobiles.   c. Horses and wagons.

4   Complete the sentences.

a. _____ has made many changes in transportation.

b. People can ride on _____ and subways today.

c. Many forms of _____ carry goods to different places.

5   Complete the outline.

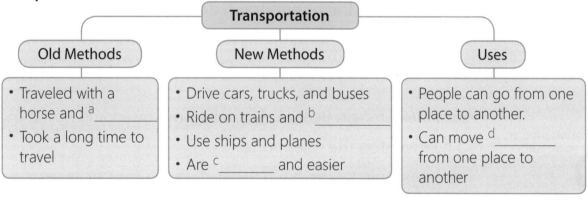

Transportation		
Old Methods	**New Methods**	**Uses**
• Traveled with a horse and ª_____ • Took a long time to travel	• Drive cars, trucks, and buses • Ride on trains and ᵇ_____ • Use ships and planes • Are ᶜ_____ and easier	• People can go from one place to another. • Can move ᵈ_____ from one place to another

Vocabulary Builder

Write the correct words and the meanings in Chinese.

▸ things for sale; products carried by trains, trucks, etc.

_____

▸ a way of moving people or goods from place to place

_____

▸ a vehicle with four wheels that is usually pulled by horses

_____

▸ a vehicle with wings and one or more engines that flies through the air

_____

Inventors and Inventions

Key Words

- inventor
- invention
- communicate
- laboratory
- invent
- phonograph
- motion picture camera
- light bulb
- be fascinated by
- sound
- electric wire

Many people like creating new things.

We call these people inventors.

And we call the new things they create inventions.

Some inventors have changed our world very much.

Some inventions have changed the way people communicate.

This is especially true for two men.

They are Thomas Edison and Alexander Graham Bell.

Thomas Edison was a famous inventor.

He worked hard in his laboratory every day.

He invented hundreds of electric things.

These included the phonograph and a motion picture camera.

Edison also invented the light bulb we use today.

Thanks to Edison, people could light their own homes.

Alexander Graham Bell was fascinated by sound and how it moved.

So he invented the telephone.

This let people talk to each other through electric wires.

Today, millions of people around the world use telephones to talk to people miles away. And it is all because of Alexander Graham Bell.

motion picture camera

Two Great Inventors

Thomas Edison

(1847–1931)

light bulb

phonograph

Alexander Graham Bell

(1847–1922)

Bell's "box telephone"

Main Idea and Details

1 **What is the main idea of the passage?**

a. Some people like to try to invent new things.

b. The telephone lets people talk to others around the world.

c. Edison and Bell changed the world with their inventions.

2 **What did Thomas Edison invent?**

a. The telephone.   b. The electric light.   c. The stereo.

3 **What does fascinated mean?**

a. Attracted.   b. Surprised.   c. Bored.

4 **According to the passage, which statement is true?**

a. Bell had more inventions than Edison did.

b. Thomas Edison made hundreds of inventions.

c. Alexander Graham Bell invented a motion picture camera.

5 **Complete the outline.**

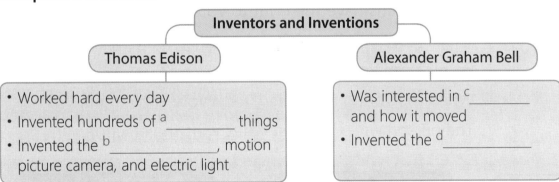

Inventors and Inventions

Thomas Edison
- Worked hard every day
- Invented hundreds of ᵃ_____ things
- Invented the ᵇ_____, motion picture camera, and electric light

Alexander Graham Bell
- Was interested in ᶜ_____ and how it moved
- Invented the ᵈ_____

Vocabulary Builder

Write the correct words and the meanings in Chinese.

1 ▸ something that is made or designed for the first time

_____

2 ▸ a camera used to make rapid exposure of moving objects

_____

3 ▸ a building or a room where a scientist does special tests and research

_____

4 ▸ the glass object in a lamp that produces light

_____

Choosing Our Leaders

 03

We live in a democracy.

So we vote for most of our government leaders.

We vote in elections.

There are many different elections.

There are local, state, and national elections in the U.S.

In these elections, people run for different offices.

In local elections, people vote for the mayor of a city.

In state elections, people vote for the governor or congressmen.

And in national elections, people vote for the president.

So who can vote?

Adult citizens have the right to vote in elections.

They must be at least 18 years old by election day.

Each citizen votes one time.

When the voting is finished, each vote is counted.

The person with the most votes wins the election.

Key Words

- democracy
- vote
- government
- election
- run for
- office
- congressman
- adult
- election day
- count

We vote for
our leaders.

In the elections, people run for different offices.

When the voting is finished, each vote is counted.

In national elections, people vote for the president.

Adult citizens over 18 have the right to vote.

BALLOT BOX

Main Idea and Details

1   What is the main idea of the passage?

a. Not everyone is allowed to vote.

b. Citizens can vote in the elections.

c. Everyone can vote for the president.

2   People can vote for the _____ in a local election.

a. mayor   b. governor   c. president

3   How old must a person be to be able to vote in the U.S.?

a. Sixteen.   b. Eighteen.   c. Twenty-one.

4   Answer the questions.

a. How do people vote? _____

b. Who do people vote for in state elections? _____

c. How many times does a person vote in an election? _____

5   Complete the outline.

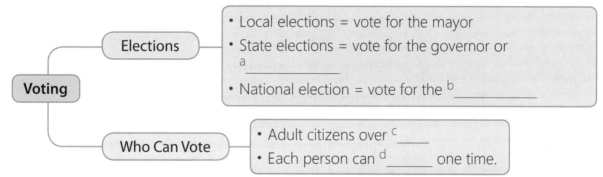

Voting

Elections
- Local elections = vote for the mayor
- State elections = vote for the governor or
  a _____
- National election = vote for the b _____

Who Can Vote
- Adult citizens over c _____
- Each person can d _____ one time.

Vocabulary Builder

Write the correct words and the meanings in Chinese.

 ▸ to choose someone or something in an election

_____

 ▸ to enter into an election contest for a particular office

_____

 ▸ fully grown and developed

_____

 ▸ to calculate the total number of things

_____

Presidents' Day in February

Key Words

- George Washington
- the father of our country
- be born
- celebrate
- birthday
- national holiday
- Abraham Lincoln
- Civil War
- free
- slave
- honor

George Washington was the first president of the United States.
Americans call him "the father of our country."
Many people call him the greatest American president.
Washington was born on February 22, 1732.
Even when he was president, Americans celebrated his birthday every year. Soon, it became a national holiday.
It was called Washington's Birthday.

Abraham Lincoln was the 16th president of the United States.
He won the Civil War and helped free black slaves.
Lincoln was born on February 12, 1809.
After Lincoln died, people wanted to honor him, too.

Some people changed the name of Washington's Birthday.
They began calling it "Presidents' Day."
This let them honor both Washington and Lincoln.

Today, Americans celebrate Presidents' Day on the third Monday in February. Schools, banks, and many offices are closed to show respect for two great American leaders.

✓ Presidents' Day Celebration

Americans honor both Washington and Lincoln in February.

Americans call Washington "the father of our country."

Lincoln won the Civil War and helped free black slaves.

14

Main Idea and Details

1 What is the passage mainly about?

a. Why we celebrate Presidents' Day.

b. How we celebrate Presidents' Day.

c. Where we celebrate Presidents' Day.

2 When was George Washington born?

a. February 12, 1809.   b. February 16, 1799.   c. February 22, 1732.

3 What does honor mean?

a. Show a picture to.   b. Show an idea to.   c. Show respect to.

4 Answer the questions.

a. What do Americans call George Washington? _____

b. When was Abraham Lincoln born? _____

c. What places are closed on Presidents' Day? _____

5 Complete the outline.

Presidents' Day

George Washington

- Was the ᵃ_____ president of the U.S.
- Is called "the ᵇ_____ of our country"
- Was born on February 22, 1732

Abraham Lincoln

- Was the 16th president of the U.S.
- Won the ᶜ_____ _____
- Freed black ᵈ_____
- Was born on February 12, 1809

Today's Celebrations

- Is on the third Monday in ᵉ_____
- Schools, banks, and many offices close.

Vocabulary Builder

Write the correct words and the meanings in Chinese.

1 ▸ the first president of the United States

_____

2 ▸ to release; to allow to live without being controlled

_____

3 ▸ the war fought in the United States between northern and southern states from 1861 to 1865

_____

4 ▸ someone who is owned by another person and works for him or her

_____

Vocabulary **Review 1**

A

Complete the sentences with the words below.

carry	way	creating	travel
light	goods	communicate	telephones

1 New technology changes the _____ people live.

2 In the past, it took days to _____ by horses and wagons.

3 Many kinds of transportation are used to _____ goods.

4 Transportation moves people and _____ from one place to another.

5 Many people like _____ new things.

6 Some inventions have changed the way people _____.

7 Thanks to Edison, people could _____ their own homes.

8 Today, people around the world use _____ to talk to people miles away.

B

Complete the sentences with the words below.

first	right	elections	Civil War
run	born	government	Presidents' Day

1 We vote for most of our _____ leaders.

2 There are local, state, and national _____ in the U.S.

3 In these elections, people _____ for different offices.

4 Adult citizens have the _____ to vote in elections.

5 George Washington was the _____ president of the United States.

6 Washington was _____ on February 22, 1732.

7 Abraham Lincoln won the _____ _____ and helped free black slaves.

8 Today, Americans celebrate _____ _____ on the third Monday in February.

C Write the correct word and the meaning in Chinese.

1 ▸ a way of moving people or goods from one place to another

_____

2 ▸ a vehicle with four wheels that is usually pulled by horses

_____

3 ▸ a building or a room where a scientist does special tests and research

_____

4 ▸ the glass object in a lamp that produces light

_____

5 ▸ the act of choosing someone for a public office by voting

_____

6 ▸ a holiday celebrated throughout a nation

_____

D Match each word with the correct definition and write the meaning in Chinese.

1 technology _____ ☐

2 subway _____ ☐

3 inventor _____ ☐

4 invent _____ ☐

5 vote _____ ☐

6 congressman _____ ☐

7 election day _____ ☐

8 count _____ ☐

9 Abraham Lincoln _____ ☐

10 free _____ ☐

a. to make something for the first time

b. a railroad that runs under the ground

c. to calculate the total number of things

d. someone who is a member of a congress

e. using science to make things faster or better

f. to choose someone or something in an election

g. someone who makes or invents something new

h. the 16th president of the U.S. who freed black slaves

i. to release; to allow to live without being controlled

j. the day when you vote in order to choose someone for office

Countries Have Neighbors

Key Words

- continent
- North America
- several
- neighbor
- touch
- Caribbean Sea
- be situated
- island
- beside
- South America

The United States is part of a continent called North America.

A continent is a very large piece of land.

In fact, the United States is not the only country in North America.

It has several neighbors.

To the north of the country is Canada.

To the south of the country is Mexico.

Both Canada and Mexico touch the U.S.

The U.S. has other neighbors, too.

The Caribbean Sea is situated to the south of it.

There are many islands in the sea.

Cuba, Haiti, and the Dominican Republic are there.

Also, to the north, Russia is beside Alaska.

Brazil and its neighbors are on the continent of South America.

Brazil is the largest country in South America.

Argentina, Chile, and Columbia are there, too.

All of these countries are America's neighbors.

Russia

Alaska

Canada

United States

Cuba

Haiti

Dominican Republic

Mexico

Caribbean Sea

Columbia

Brazil

Chile

Argentina

The U.S. has many neighbors in North and South America.

Canada

Mexico

Caribbean Sea

Brazil

Chile

Cuba

Main Idea and Details

1 What is the main idea of the passage?

a. The U.S., Mexico, and Canada are in North America.

b. There are many countries near the United States.

c. There are many countries in South America.

2 The Caribbean Sea is _____ of the United States.

a. north   b. south   c. west

3 Which country touches the United States?

a. Mexico.   b. Cuba.   c. Russia.

4 According to the passage, which statement is true?

a. The United States is in South America.

b. Russia is beside Cuba.

c. Argentina is in South America.

5 Complete the outline.

The United States Has Neighbors

North America
- Canada and Mexico touch the U.S.
- Cuba, Haiti, and the ᵃ_____ Republic are there.
- ᵇ_____ is beside Alaska.

South America
- It is to the south of the U.S.
- ᶜ_____ is the largest country.
- Argentina, ᵈ_____, and Columbia are there.

Vocabulary Builder

Write the correct words and the meanings in Chinese.

 ▸ a very large piece of land

_____

 ▸ the part of the Atlantic Ocean between North and South America

_____

 ▸ next to (someone or something)

_____

 ▸ to be located

_____

Unit 06

The Amazon Rain Forest

Key Words

- be located
- flow
- surround
- enormous
- rain forest
- jungle
- amazing
- species
- mammal
- tropical bird
- cut down
- destroy

The Amazon River is the world's second longest river.
It is located in South America.
It flows mostly in Brazil, but it goes through seven other countries, too.
Surrounding the Amazon River is an enormous rain forest.
It is the Amazon rain forest.

The Amazon rain forest is the largest jungle in the world.
Inside it, there is an amazing amount of life.
Around half of all of the world's animal species live there.
Over 500 species of mammals, almost 500 types of reptiles, and huge numbers of tropical birds live there.
Scientists think around 30 million species of insects live there.
There are a wide variety of trees, plants, and flowers, too.

Today, however, some of the Amazon rain forest is getting cut down.
This is making the rain forest smaller, which is destroying the home of many plants and animals.
We need to protect the Amazon.
Without the rain forest, millions of plants and animals would die.

The Amazon rain forest is home to many plants and animals.

Deforestation in the Amazon

Main Idea and Details

1   What is the passage mainly about?

   a. The Amazon River.

   b. The Amazon rain forest.

   c. Brazil and South America.

2   About how many species of mammals live in the Amazon rain forest?

   a. 50   **b.** 500   **c.** 30 million.

3   What does enormous mean?

   a. Rainy.   **b.** Dangerous.   **c.** Huge.

4   Answer the questions.

   a. Where does the Amazon River flow? _____

   b. Around how many species of insects live in the Amazon rain forest? _____

   c. What could happen without the rain forest? _____

5   Complete the outline.

The Amazon Rain Forest

Location
- Beside the Amazon River
- In Brazil and ᵃ_____ other countries in South America

Animals and Plants
- Around half of all of the world's ᵇ_____
- 500 species of mammals and reptiles
- Many tropical birds
- 30 million species of ᶜ_____
- A wide variety of plants

Problems
- People are cutting it down.
- People are ᵈ_____ the home of many plants and animals there.

Vocabulary Builder

Write the correct words and the meanings in Chinese.

1  ▶ a group of animals or plants that are similar

_____

2  ▶ a tropical forest that receives a lot of rain

_____

3 ▶ a thick tropical forest

_____

4  ▶ to cut a tree so that it falls to the ground; to destroy

_____

Protecting the Earth

There are many kinds of natural resources on the earth.
We use natural resources every day.
Air, water, soil, plants, and animals are some important resources we use. Without them, we would not be able to survive.

People have changed the earth in many ways.
We cut down trees to build homes and buildings.
We make dams to hold water.
We pave roads and construct bridges.
We dig in the ground to find fuels such as coal, oil, and gas.

However, we need to be careful about the changes we make.
Some changes could cause problems to the earth.
If we cut down too many trees, animals must find new homes and food.
If they cannot do these things, they will die.
When we make pollution, we harm natural resources.
If the water and air are not clean, we cannot use them.
Plants and animals could also die.
We need to use fewer resources and protect more plants and animals.

Key Words

- natural resource
- dam
- pave
- construct
- dig
- fuel
- coal
- pollution
- harm

People Change the Earth

building dams

cutting down trees

constructing bridges

digging up fuels

paving roads

Main Idea and Details

1 **What is the main idea of the passage?**

   a. We must protect the earth as we change it.

   b. Too much pollution can kill lots of animals.

   c. Paving roads and building bridges change the land.

2 **People might dig in the ground to find _____.**

   a. dams   **b.** plants   **c.** fuels

3 **What can pollution do?**

   a. Harm natural resources.

   b. Make people healthier.

   c. Help clean the air and water.

4 **Answer the questions.**

   a. What are some important resources that people use? _____

   b. Why do people make dams? _____

   c. What should we use fewer of? _____

5 **Complete the outline.**

Earth

Natural Resources
- Air, water, soil, plants, and ᵃ_____
- Need them to survive

Changes We Make
- Cut down trees
- Make ᵇ_____
- Pave roads
- Construct bridges
- Dig in the ᶜ_____ to find fuels

Problems
- Animals need to find new ᵈ_____ and food.
- Pollution
- Dirty water and air
- Plants and animals could die.

Vocabulary Builder

Write the correct words and the meanings in Chinese.

1 ▸ a wall built across a river in order to hold water

_____

2 ▸ a substance such as coal or oil that can be burned to produce energy

_____

3 ▸ to cover a piece of ground with concrete, stones, or bricks

_____

4 ▸ to move soil, sand, snow, etc., in order to create a hole

_____

Key Words

- endangered
- California condor
- giant panda
- Bengal tiger
- blue whale
- loggerhead turtle
- national park
- watch
- hunting
- prohibit

There are millions of animals all over the world.

But some kinds of animals are endangered.

This means that very few of these animals are living.

If people do not protect them, they may all die.

Today, there are over 40,000 endangered species.

These animals live in many countries.

The California condor, a huge bird, is an endangered animal in the United States.

The giant panda in China is endangered, too.

So is the Bengal tiger in India.

Even animals in the oceans are endangered.

The blue whale in the Pacific Ocean and the loggerhead turtle in the Atlantic Ocean are two of these.

People are finding ways to protect many endangered animals.

Some endangered animals live in national parks and are being watched carefully.

The hunting of endangered animals is strictly prohibited by laws.

Some Endangered Animals

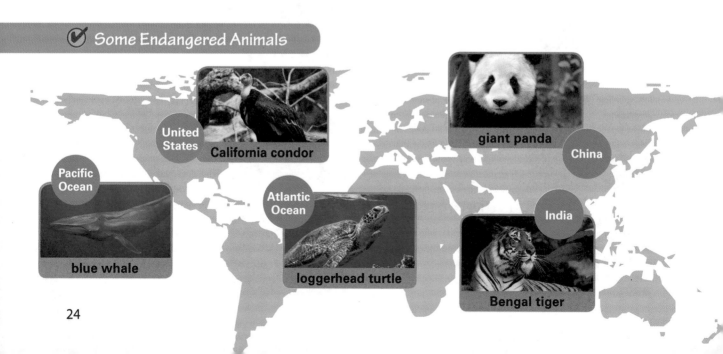

United States — California condor
giant panda — China
Pacific Ocean — blue whale
Atlantic Ocean — loggerhead turtle
India — Bengal tiger

Main Idea and Details

1   What is the passage mainly about?

a. Animals in the ocean.

b. Some endangered animals.

c. Hunting endangered animals.

2   What is an endangered animal in India?

a. The panda.   b. The California condor.   c. The Bengal tiger.

3   What does prohibited **mean?**

a. Not allowed.   b. Requested.   c. Permitted.

4   Complete the sentences.

a. Around _____ animal species on the earth are endangered.

b. The blue whale lives in the _____ _____ .

c. People may not _____ endangered animals.

5   Complete the outline.

The World's Endangered Species

Animals

• California condor: U.S.
• Giant panda: a_____
• Bengal tiger: India
• b_____ _____ : Pacific Ocean
• Loggerhead turtle: Atlantic Ocean

Protecting Animals

• Live in c_____ parks
• Are watched carefully
• d_____ is prohibited.

Vocabulary Builder

Write the correct words and the meanings in Chinese.

 ▸ being in danger of extinction

_____

 ▸ a large sea turtle in the Atlantic Ocean

_____

 ▸ an area of land protected by a national government for its natural beauty or the preservation of wildlife

_____

 ▸ to ban; not to allow

_____

A

Complete the sentences with the words below.

Caribbean Sea	neighbors	longest	variety
South America	enormous	touch	species

1   The United States has several _____.

2   Both Canada and Mexico _____ the U.S.

3   The _____ _____ is situated to the south of the U.S.

4   Brazil and its neighbors are on the continent of _____ _____.

5   The Amazon River is the world's second _____ river.

6   Surrounding the Amazon River is an _____ rain forest.

7   Around half of all of the world's animal _____ live in the Amazon rain forest.

8   There are a wide _____ of trees, plants, and flowers, too.

B

Complete the sentences with the words below.

changed	problems	protect	clean
strictly	resources	endangered	pave

1   There are many kinds of natural _____ on the earth.

2   People have _____ the earth in many ways.

3   We _____ roads and construct bridges.

4   Some changes could cause _____ to the earth.

5   If the water and air are not _____, we cannot use them.

6   Some kinds of animals are _____.

7   People are finding ways to _____ many endangered animals.

8   The hunting of endangered animals is _____ prohibited by laws.

C

Write the correct word and the meaning in Chinese.

 ▸ an area of thick forest where it rains a lot; a tropical forest

_____

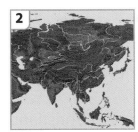 ▸ a very large piece of land

_____

 ▸ a wall built across a river in order to hold water

_____

 ▸ the process of polluting the water, air, or land; dirty substances that pollute a place

_____

 ▸ a type of animal that feeds milk to its young

_____

 ▸ the chasing or killing of wild animals

_____

D

Match each word with the correct definition and write the meaning in Chinese.

1 several _____ ☐

2 touch _____ ☐

3 be situated _____ ☐

4 surround _____ ☐

5 amazing _____ ☐

6 cut down _____ ☐

7 pollution _____ ☐

8 harm _____ ☐

9 endangered _____ ☐

10 prohibit _____ ☐

a. to border
b. to be located
c. to ban; not to allow
d. being in danger of extinction
e. to damage or hurt something
f. making someone feel very surprised
g. to be all around something; to enclose
h. being of a number more than two but not many
i. to cut a tree so that it falls to the ground; to destroy
j. the process of polluting the water, air, or land; dirty substances that pollute a place

World Religions

There are many religions in the world.
The followers of most religions believe in a god or gods.

Key Words

- religion
- follower
- Christianity
- Christian
- Bible
- Buddhism
- Buddhist
- Islam
- prophet
- Muslim
- Hinduism
- Hindu

Followers of Christianity believe that Jesus Christ is the son of God.
They are called Christians.
Christians have a holy book called the Bible.
Christians go to church on Sunday and on other special days.

Followers of Buddhism do not believe in any gods.
They are called Buddhists.
Buddhists believe that they return to life after they die.
Many Buddhists live in Asia.

Followers of Islam believe that Muhammad was a prophet of Allah.
Allah is the name of the Islamic god.
Believers in Islam are called Muslims.

Followers of Hinduism believe in one god and in many gods.
For Hindus, the one god is called Brahma.
But they believe that there are also thousands of different gods
who are like different faces or names of Brahma.

The World's Four Major Religions

Christianity

Buddhism

Islam

Hinduism

Main Idea and Details

1   What is the passage mainly about?
a. Followers of Christianity.
b. Buddhism and Islam.
c. The world's major religions.

2   How many gods are there in Hinduism?
a. One.   b. Three.   c. Thousands.

3   What does followers mean?
a. Muslims.   b. Believers.   c. Christians.

4   Complete the sentences.
a. The Christian holy book is called the _____.
b. _____ do not believe in any gods.
c. Brahma is a god in _____ .

5   Complete the outline.

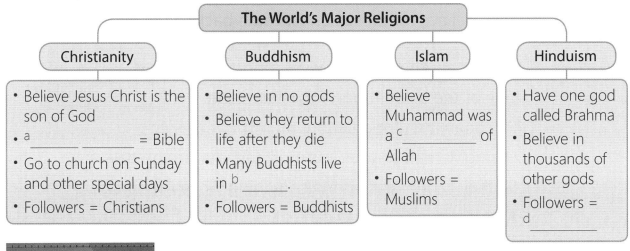

The World's Major Religions

Christianity
- Believe Jesus Christ is the son of God
- a _____ _____ = Bible
- Go to church on Sunday and other special days
- Followers = Christians

Buddhism
- Believe in no gods
- Believe they return to life after they die
- Many Buddhists live in b _____.
- Followers = Buddhists

Islam
- Believe Muhammad was a c _____ of Allah
- Followers = Muslims

Hinduism
- Have one god called Brahma
- Believe in thousands of other gods
- Followers = d _____

Vocabulary Builder

Write the correct words and the meanings in Chinese.

1 ▸ the holy book of Christianity

_____

2 ▸ the creator god in Hinduism

_____

3 ▸ a follower of Buddhism

_____

4 ▸ a follower of Islam

_____

Religious Holidays

Every religion has holidays.

They are often called holy days.

Christianity has several holy days.

The two most important days are Christmas and Easter.

Christmas is celebrated on December 25 every year.

On Christmas, Christians celebrate the birth of Jesus Christ.

Many Christians go to church and worship on Christmas.

Easter is the other major Christian holy day.

Easter is celebrated in late March or early April every year.

On Easter, Christians celebrate the Resurrection of Jesus Christ.

They believe that Jesus Christ came back to life on Easter.

Islam is another religion with important holidays.

One of the most important is Ramadan.

Ramadan lasts for an entire month.

During Ramadan, Muslims must fast during the day.

So they cannot eat or drink anything while the sun is up.

After the sun sets, they can eat.

Key Words

- holy day
- Christmas
- Easter
- worship
- Resurrection
- come back to life
- Ramadan
- last
- fast

On Christmas

On Easter

During Ramadan

Christians go to church and worship.

Christians celebrate the birth of Christ.

Christians celebrate the Resurrection of Christ.

Muslims fast from dawn until sunset.

Main Idea and Details

1 **What is the main idea of the passage?**

a. Christmas is an important day to Christians.

b. Christianity and Islam have holy days.

c. Muslims fast during the day during Ramadan.

2 **What event happened on Easter?**

a. The birth of Jesus Christ.

b. The death of Jesus Christ.

c. The Resurrection of Jesus Christ.

3 **What does fast mean?**

a. Not eat.　　　　b. Not sleep.　　　　c. Not exercise.

4 **According to the passage, which statement is true?**

a. Christmas is celebrated on December 25.

b. Easter is always during late March.

c. Ramadan lasts for two weeks.

5 **Complete the outline.**

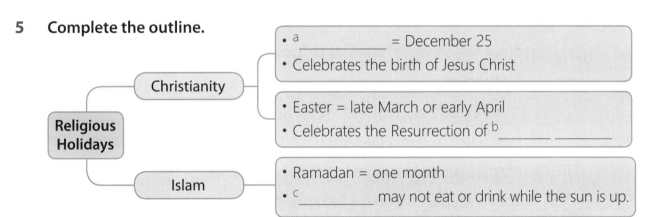

Religious Holidays

Christianity
- a _____ = December 25
- Celebrates the birth of Jesus Christ
- Easter = late March or early April
- Celebrates the Resurrection of b _____ _____

Islam
- Ramadan = one month
- c _____ may not eat or drink while the sun is up.

Vocabulary Builder

Write the correct words and the meanings in Chinese.

▶ to feel or show respect and love for a god

_____

▶ a Christian holiday to celebrate Christ's return to life

_____

▶ the coming back to life of Christ after his death

_____

▶ an Islamic holiday during which no food may be eaten during the day

_____

Early Travelers to America

The first people to live in North America were Native Americans.
Many years later, explorers came from Europe.

Key Words

- Native American
- explorer
- sail
- captain
- journey
- discover
- New World
- European
- Spaniard

One early explorer was Christopher Columbus.
In 1492, he sailed from Spain to find gold and other riches.
He was the captain of three ships, called the *Pinta*, *Niña*, and *Santa María*.
It was a long journey, but he finally found land.
He was looking for India, but he never got there.
Instead, he discovered the New World: North and South America.

After Columbus, many Europeans began sailing to the Americas.
They came from many countries.
They sailed from Spain, Portugal, France, Britain, and the Netherlands.
John Cabot of England was one explorer.
He sailed around Canada.
Many Spaniards sailed to the New World.
They included Vasco de Balboa, Ponce de León, and Hernando Cortés.
Every year, more and more men came to the New World.

☑ Early Explorers to America

Santa María

Niña

Pinta

Christopher Columbus

John Cabot

Vasco de Balboa

Ponce de León

Hernando Cortés

Main Idea and Details

1 **What is the main idea of the passage?**

a. John Cabot and Vasco de Balboa visited the New World.

b. Christopher Columbus was the first European to visit North America.

c. Many explorers visited North America after Christopher Columbus.

2 **Columbus's ships were the *Pinta*, *Niña*, and _____.**

a. *Santa Claus*   **b.** *Santa María*   **c.** *Santa Michelle*

3 **Which country sent many explorers to the New World?**

a. England.   **b.** France.   **c.** Spain.

4 **According to the passage, which statement is true?**

a. Christopher Columbus sailed to the New World in 1491.

b. Europeans from Spain, Russia, and Poland sailed to the New World.

c. Ponce de León and Hernando Cortés sailed to the New World from Spain.

5 **Complete the outline.**

> **European Explorers of the New World**

> **Christopher Columbus**
> - Sailed from ᵃ_____ in 1492
> - 3 ships = *Pinta*, *Niña*, and *Santa María*
> - Was looking for India
> - Found the ᵇ_____ _____ instead

> **Other Explorers**
> - Sailed from Spain, Portugal, France, Britain, and the Netherlands
> - ᶜ_____ : John Cabot
> - ᵈ_____ : Vasco de Balboa, Ponce de León, and Hernando Cortés

Vocabulary Builder

Write the correct words and the meanings in Chinese.

1  ▸ someone who travels to places that little is known about

_____

2  ▸ someone who commands a ship

_____

3  ▸ to travel on water in a ship or boat

_____

4  ▸ North and South America

_____

The Pilgrims and Thanksgiving

 12

Key Words

- Pilgrim
- Church of England
- religious
- disagree
- worship
- *Mayflower*
- land
- settlement
- Wampanoag
- Thanksgiving

The Pilgrims were a religious group of people in England.

They disagreed with the Church of England.

They wanted to worship God in their own way.

So, they decided to leave England to look for religious freedom.

In 1620, the Pilgrims left England to come to America.

They sailed on a ship called the *Mayflower*.

They landed in an area of America called Massachusetts.

The Pilgrims built a settlement there called Plymouth.

Their first winter was very hard. 40 people died that winter.

The Pilgrims did not know how to live in their new home.

But Wampanoag Indians saved them.

They showed the Pilgrims how to fish, hunt, and grow food.

By fall, the Pilgrims had lots of food and a successful settlement in America.

The Pilgrims invited the Native Americans to a meal.

They thanked God for all of the good things they had.

It was the first Thanksgiving.

 The Pilgrims

The First Thanksgiving

the Pilgrims departing on the *Mayflower*

The Pilgrims and the Native Americans celebrated the first Thanksgiving together.

Main Idea and Details

1   What is the passage mainly about?

   a. The first Thanksgiving.

   b. The Pilgrims and their lives in America.

   c. Sailing to Plymouth on the *Mayflower*.

2   What did the Wampanoag Indians do for the Pilgrims?

   a. They taught them how to fish, hunt, and grow food.

   b. They taught them how to build nice houses.

   c. They taught them how to cook their food.

3   What does landed mean?

   a. Arrived.   **b.** Found.   **c.** Lived.

4   Complete the sentences.

   a. The Pilgrims wanted religious _____, so they left England.

   b. The Pilgrims went to America in _____.

   c. The Pilgrims had the first _____ with the Native Americans.

5   Complete the outline.

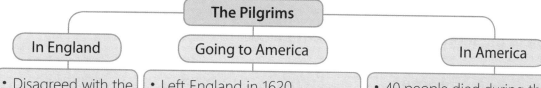

The Pilgrims

In England
- Disagreed with the Church of England
- Wanted religious
  a _____

Going to America
- Left England in 1620
- Sailed on a ship called the *Mayflower*
- b _____ in Massachusetts

In America
- 40 people died during the first winter.
- Learned much from the Wampanoag c _____
- Built a successful settlement
- Had the first d _____ with the Native Americans

Vocabulary Builder

Write the correct words and the meanings in Chinese.

1 ▸ the national church of England

_____

2 ▸ relating to religion

_____

3 ▸ a group of people from England who sailed to America on the *Mayflower*

_____

4 ▸ a place people live, especially where no one has lived before; a settling in a new place

_____

Review 3

A

Complete the sentences with the words below.

prophet	fast	religions	Resurrection
holidays	life	celebrated	Brahma

1   The followers of most _____ believe in a god or gods.

2   Followers of Islam believe that Muhammad was a _____ of Allah.

3   For Hindus, the one god is called _____.

4   Buddhists believe that they return to _____ after they die.

5   Every religion has _____.

6   Christmas is _____ on December 25 every year.

7   On Easter, Christians celebrate the _____ of Jesus Christ.

8   During Ramadan, Muslims must _____ during the day.

B

Complete the sentences with the words below.

Native Americans	Europe	sailing	invited
New World	how to	landed	Pilgrims

1   The first people to live in North America were _____ _____.

2   Many years later, explorers came from _____.

3   Columbus discovered the _____ _____: North and South America.

4   After Columbus, many Europeans began _____ to the Americas.

5   The _____ were a religious group of people in England.

6   The Pilgrims _____ in an area of America called Massachusetts.

7   Wampanoag Indians showed the Pilgrims _____ _____ fish, hunt, and grow food.

8   The Pilgrims _____ the Native Americans to a meal.

Write the correct word and the meaning in Chinese.

1 ▸ a group of people from England who sailed to America on the *Mayflower*

_____

2 ▸ a follower of Christianity

_____

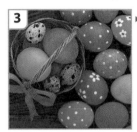
3 ▸ a Christian holiday to celebrate Christ's return to life

_____

4 ▸ an Islamic holiday during which no food may be eaten during the day

_____

5 ▸ someone who travels to places that little is known about

_____

6 ▸ someone who commands a ship

_____

D

Match each word with the correct definition and write the meaning in Chinese.

1 Resurrection _____ ☐

2 Christian _____ ☐

3 Muslim _____ ☐

4 worship _____ ☐

5 journey _____ ☐

6 Spaniard _____ ☐

7 disagree _____ ☐

8 religious _____ ☐

9 *Mayflower* _____ ☐

10 settlement _____ ☐

a. a follower of Islam

b. a follower of Christianity

c. relating to religion

d. a long-distance trip

e. the ship that the Pilgrims sailed on

f. to have a different opinion; to quarrel

g. to show respect to God, especially by praying in a church

h. a Spanish citizen; a person of Spanish origin

i. the coming back to life of Christ after his death

j. a place people live, especially where no one has lived before; a settling in a new place

Wrap-Up Test 1

A

Write the correct word for each sentence.

> religious endangered religions North America resources
> inventions surrounding elections transportation celebrate

1 Many kinds of _____ are used to carry goods.

2 Some _____ have changed the way people communicate.

3 There are local, state, and national _____ in the U.S.

4 People are finding ways to protect many _____ animals.

5 There are many kinds of natural _____ on the earth.

6 _____ the Amazon River is an enormous rain forest.

7 The followers of most _____ believe in a god or gods.

8 The first people to live in _____ _____ were Native Americans.

9 On Easter, Christians _____ the Resurrection of Jesus Christ.

10 The Pilgrims were a _____ group of people in England.

B

Write the meanings of the words in Chinese.

1	transportation	_____	16	amazing	_____
2	laboratory	_____	17	cut down	_____
3	slave	_____	18	pollution	_____
4	technology	_____	19	endangered	_____
5	inventor	_____	20	prohibit	_____
6	vote	_____	21	Bible	_____
7	congressman	_____	22	Buddhist	_____
8	election	_____	23	Easter	_____
9	count	_____	24	explorer	_____
10	free	_____	25	Resurrection	_____
11	rain forest	_____	26	Muslim	_____
12	fuel	_____	27	worship	_____
13	touch	_____	28	Spaniard	_____
14	be situated	_____	29	follower	_____
15	surround	_____	30	settlement	_____

2

● Science

We live on the earth's surface.

However, beneath us, the earth has several different layers.

They are the crust, mantle, and core.

The crust is the thin outermost layer of the earth.

That's the surface of the earth that we live on.

All of the earth's water and land—mountains, rivers, oceans, and continents—make up the earth's crust.

The mantle is the rock layer below the crust.

It is the earth's thickest layer and is full of hot melted rock.

In fact, the mantle is very hot.

The deeper the mantle, the hotter it gets.

At the center of the earth is the core.

There are two parts: the outer core and the inner core.

The outer core is extremely hot and is mostly liquid metal.

The inner core is mostly solid iron and nickel.

Key Words

- surface
- beneath
- layer
- crust
- mantle
- core
- outermost
- melted rock
- extremely
- liquid metal

The earth has several different layers.

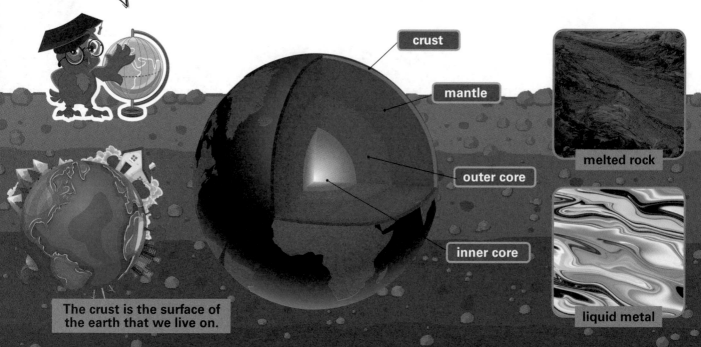

crust

mantle

outer core

inner core

melted rock

liquid metal

The crust is the surface of the earth that we live on.

Main Idea and Details

1 **What is the passage mainly about?**

   a. The two parts of the core.

   b. The size of the crust and mantle.

   c. The different layers of the earth.

2 **The _____ layer of the earth is the crust.**

   a. thickest   **b.** middle   **c.** outermost

3 **What is the mantle full of?**

   a. Melted rock.   **b.** Iron and nickel.

   c. Mountains, rivers, oceans, and continents.

4 **Complete the sentences.**

   a. The layers of the earth are the crust, mantle, and _____.

   b. The temperature in the mantle is very _____.

   c. The outer core is mostly _____ metal.

5 **Complete the outline.**

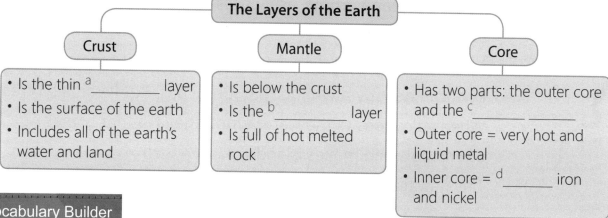

The Layers of the Earth

Crust
- Is the thin ^{a}_____ layer
- Is the surface of the earth
- Includes all of the earth's water and land

Mantle
- Is below the crust
- Is the ^{b}_____ layer
- Is full of hot melted rock

Core
- Has two parts: the outer core and the ^{c}_____ _____
- Outer core = very hot and liquid metal
- Inner core = ^{d}_____ iron and nickel

Vocabulary Builder

Write the correct words and the meanings in Chinese.

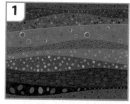 **1** ▸ a covering piece of material that lies over or under another

_____

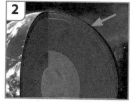 **2** ▸ the surface of the earth

_____

 **3** ▸ the rock layer below the crust

_____

 **4** ▸ metal in the form of liquid

_____

Earthquakes and Volcanoes

Key Words

- shaking
- last
- earthquake
- underground
- violent
- crack
- burst
- volcano
- magma
- erupt
- ash
- lava

Sometimes, the ground begins shaking.

This shaking can last for a few seconds or several minutes.

This is an earthquake.

Earthquakes happen when parts of the crust move underground.

Most earthquakes are not powerful, but some are very violent.

They can crack roads and destroy buildings.

Earthquakes can also change the earth's surface.

They can cause the land to fall or rise.

In some places, hot melted rock bursts out of the ground.

This is a volcano.

The hot melted rock, called magma, comes from the mantle.

When a volcano erupts, ash, gases, and magma flow onto the earth's surface.

Magma is called lava when it reaches the earth's surface.

Lava can destroy anything that it touches. But it can also create.

When volcanoes in the water erupt, the lava that comes out often cools and makes islands.

The Hawaiian Islands were formed this way by volcanoes.

Earthquakes can be very violent.

The Eruption of a Volcano

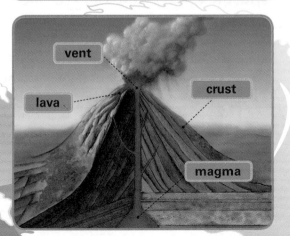

vent

lava

crust

magma

Main Idea and Details

1   What is the main idea of the passage?
   a. Volcanoes and earthquakes can affect the earth.
   b. Volcanoes and earthquakes can kill many people.
   c. Volcanoes and earthquakes can destroy the land.

2   How can earthquakes change the earth's surface?
   a. They can make lakes and rivers.
   b. They can create new islands.
   c. They can make the land rise or fall.

3   What does erupts mean?
   a. Makes.   b. Explodes.   c. Attacks.

4   According to the passage, which statement is true?
   a. Earthquakes formed the Hawaiian Islands.
   b. Earthquakes always last for several minutes.
   c. Ash, gas, and lava come from volcanoes.

5   Complete the outline.

Earthquakes
• Are the shaking of the ᵃ_____ for seconds or minutes
• Parts of crust move underground.
• Can be violent
• May destroy buildings and roads
• Can make the land rise or ᵇ_____

Volcanoes
• Are places where hot ᶜ_____ _____ comes from the ground
• Send out ash, gas, and magma
• ᵈ_____ destroys anything it touches.
• Can make islands like the Hawaiian Islands

Vocabulary Builder

Write the correct words and the meanings in Chinese.

► to break (something) so that there are lines in its surface
_____

► the shaking of the earth's surface
_____

► to send out rocks, ash, lava, etc., in a sudden explosion
_____

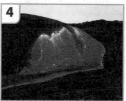
► hot melted rock that flows from a volcano onto the earth's surface
_____

Why Does the Moon Seem to Change?

 15

The largest object in the night sky is the moon.
But the moon's appearance seems to change every day.
Sometimes we can see all or part of it.
Sometimes we cannot see it at all.

In fact, the moon does not change its shape.
The moon is a huge ball of rock that moves around Earth.
The moon does not make its own light like stars do.
It looks bright because it reflects light from the sun.
As the moon orbits Earth, the lit part of the moon
that we can see changes each night.
This is why the moon seems to change shape.

The different moon shapes are called the phases of the moon.
The four main phases of the moon are new moon, first quarter,
full moon, and last quarter.
It takes about 29 days for the moon to go through all of its phases.

Key Words

- object
- appearance
- bright
- reflect
- orbit
- lit
- phase
- new moon
- first quarter
- full moon
- last quarter

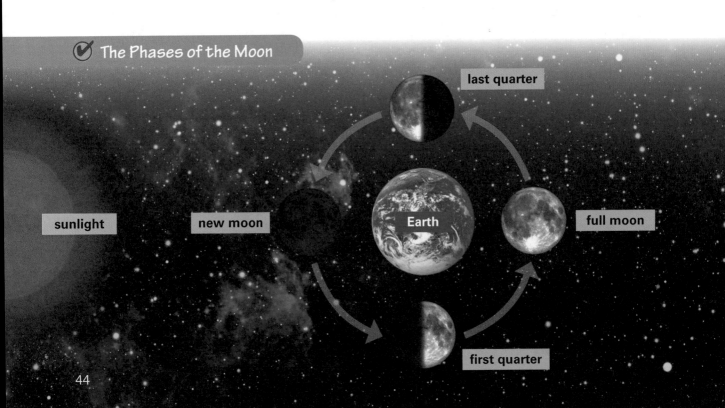

The Phases of the Moon

sunlight

new moon

Earth

last quarter

full moon

first quarter

Main Idea and Details

1   What is the main idea of the passage?

a. The moon has four main phases.

b. The moon seems to change its shape as it orbits Earth.

c. We can see the moon from Earth.

2   The moon goes through its _____ in 29 days.

a. phases   b. orbit   c. reflection

3   Why does the moon look bright?

a. It can make its own light.   b. It reflects the sun's light.

c. There is bright light on Earth.

4   Answer the questions.

a. What is the moon? _____

b. What are the different shapes of the moon called? _____

c. What are the four main phases of the moon? _____

5   Complete the outline.

The Moon

Appearance
- Seems to change every day
- Does not change its shape
- Can be seen because of the ᵃ_____ _____
- Changes appearance as it orbits ᵇ_____

Phases
- Has four main phases: new moon, first quarter, full moon, and
  ᶜ_____ _____
- Goes through all of its phases in 29 days

Vocabulary Builder

Write the correct words and the meanings in Chinese.

 1 ▸ a shape of the moon as we see it from the Earth at different times in the month
_____

 2 ▸ to send back the light from the surface
_____

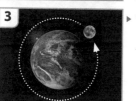 3 ▸ to move around
_____

 4 ▸ one of the four main phases of the moon, occurring between full moon and new moon
_____

The First Man on the Moon

 16

Key Words

• satellite
• outer space
• Space Race
• declaration
• space program
• launch
• lunar
• mission
• NASA
• astronaut

On October 4, 1957, the Soviet Union sent a satellite into outer space. This began the Space Race between the Soviet Union and the United States.

Then, in 1961, President John F. Kennedy made a declaration. He declared that America would send a man to the moon before the 1960s ended.
The American space program began sending many men into space after that.

Finally, in 1969, the United States was ready to visit the moon.
On July 16, *Apollo 11* was launched from the Kennedy Space Center.
It was the third lunar mission of NASA's Apollo Program.
Four days later, on July 20, the *Apollo 11* mission landed the first humans on the moon.
Neil Armstrong and Buzz Aldrin became the first humans to walk on the moon.
Astronaut Michael Collins stayed in orbit around the moon.
On July 24, all three men returned home safely.

✓ The *Apollo 11* Lunar Mission

Neil Armstrong
the first man on the moon

Buzz Aldrin

Main Idea and Details

1 **What is the passage mainly about?**

a. *Apollo 11*.

b. President John F. Kennedy.

c. The first humans on the moon.

2 **Which astronaut on *Apollo 11* did not walk on the moon?**

a. Michael Collins. b. Neil Armstrong. c. Buzz Aldrin.

3 **What does Race mean?**

a. Competition. b. Game. c. War.

4 **Complete the sentences.**

a. The Space Race was between the Soviet Union and the _____ _____.

b. President _____ wanted to send a man to the moon.

c. _____ _____ landed on the moon on July 20, 1969.

5 **Complete the outline.**

The First Man on the Moon

The Space Race
- Started in 1957
- Was between the
  a _____
  and the United States

President Kennedy
- Made a declaration
- Wanted to put a man on the b _____ by the end of the 1960s

Apollo 11
- c _____ on July 16
- Landed on the moon on July 20
- Neil Armstrong and Buzz Aldrin d _____ on the moon.
- Michael Collins stayed in orbit around the moon.

Vocabulary Builder

Write the correct words and the meanings in Chinese.

 **1** ▶ of or relating to the moon

_____

 **2** ▶ a task or job that someone is given to do

_____

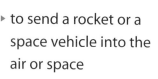 **3** ▶ to send a rocket or a space vehicle into the air or space

_____

 **4** ▶ a person who is trained for traveling in a spacecraft

_____

A

Complete the sentences with the words below.

core	solid	layer	melted rock
lava	surface	erupts	underground

1   The crust is the thin outermost _____ of the earth.

2   The mantle is the earth's thickest layer and is full of hot _____ _____.

3   At the center of the earth is the _____.

4   The inner core is mostly _____ iron and nickel.

5   Earthquakes happen when parts of the crust move _____.

6   Earthquakes can change the earth's _____.

7   When a volcano _____, ash, gases, and magma flow onto the earth's surface.

8   Magma is called _____ when it reaches the earth's surface.

B

Complete the sentences with the words below.

reflects	lunar	ball	phases
space	object	humans	Space Center

1   The largest _____ in the night sky is the moon.

2   The moon is a huge _____ of rock that moves around Earth.

3   The moon looks bright because it _____ light from the sun.

4   The different moon shapes are called the _____ of the moon.

5   The American space program began sending many men into _____.

6   On July 16, *Apollo 11* was launched from the Kennedy _____ _____.

7   It was the third _____ mission of NASA's Apollo Program.

8   Neil Armstrong and Buzz Aldrin became the first _____ to walk on the moon.

C

Write the correct word and the meaning in Chinese.

1 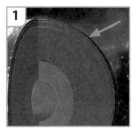 ▸ the surface of the earth

_____

2 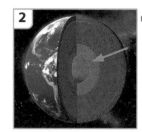 ▸ the very hot and liquid metal layer of the earth

_____

3  ▸ the shaking of the earth's surface

_____

4  ▸ a mountain with a hole in the top that sends out rocks, ash or lava in a sudden explosion

_____

5  ▸ a machine launched to orbit Earth or another planet and which is used for electronic communication

_____

6  ▸ the moon when it appears as a bright circle

_____

D

Match each word with the correct definition and write the meaning in Chinese.

1 outermost _____ ☐

2 mantle _____ ☐

3 last _____ ☐

4 violent _____ ☐

5 appearance _____ ☐

6 reflect _____ ☐

7 orbit _____ ☐

8 full moon _____ ☐

9 outer space _____ ☐

10 launch _____ ☐

a. to move around

b. farthest from the center

c. the rock layer below the crust

d. to send back the light from the surface

e. the way something or someone looks

f. the moon when it looks completely round

g. to continue for a particular length of time

h. to send a rocket or a space vehicle into the air or space

i. caused by a lot of force; using extreme physical force

j. the space outside Earth's air where the planets and stars are

Electricity

Electricity is a form of energy.

It provides power for many things to work.

Thanks to electricity, light bulbs glow, and radios play music.

Telephones use electricity to carry sound.

You need electricity to run your computer and TV.

Without electricity, many things we use every day would not work.

An electric current runs through a wire.

Wires carry electricity into your home and school.

Electricity moves from outlets, through plugs and wires,

into electric machines.

When you turn on a light at home, you are letting

electricity flow through wires to the light bulb.

You can also get electricity from batteries.

A flashlight needs electricity to work.

But you don't need to plug it into outlets.

Instead, you just put batteries inside it.

A battery can store energy inside it and change the

energy into electricity.

Key Words

- electricity
- light bulb
- glow
- radio
- electric current
- wire
- outlet
- plug
- turn on
- battery
- flashlight
- store

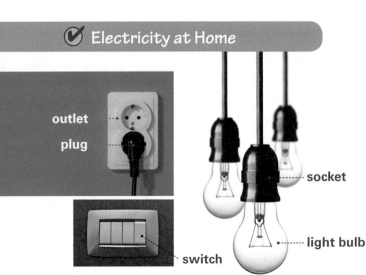

✓ Electricity at Home

outlet
plug
socket
light bulb
switch

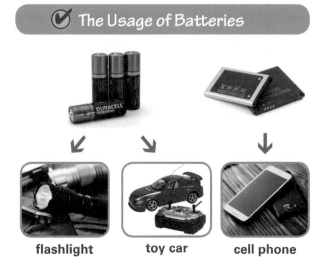

✓ The Usage of Batteries

flashlight   toy car   cell phone

Main Idea and Details

1 **What is the passage mainly about?**

    a. Electricity and how to get it.

    b. The best way to use batteries.

    c. Electric sockets, plugs, and wires.

2 **Flashlights need _____ in order to work.**

    a. wires   **b.** batteries   **c.** plugs

3 **What moves through a wire?**

    a. A plug.   **b.** An electric current.   **c.** A battery.

4 **According to the passage, which statement is true?**

    a. Light bulbs use electricity.

    b. Batteries flow through plugs.

    c. A battery can make energy.

5 **Complete the outline.**

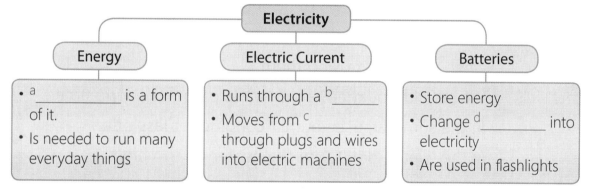

Electricity

Energy
- a _____ is a form of it.
- Is needed to run many everyday things

Electric Current
- Runs through a b_____
- Moves from c_____ through plugs and wires into electric machines

Batteries
- Store energy
- Change d_____ into electricity
- Are used in flashlights

Vocabulary Builder

Write the correct words and the meanings in Chinese.

1 ▸ to shine with a gentle, steady light

_____

2  ▸ a string-like piece of metal used to carry an electric current

_____

3  ▸ a device in a wall into which an electric cord can be plugged

_____

4  ▸ a part at the end of an electric cord that connects the cord to a source of electricity

_____

Conserving Electricity

Refrigerators, TVs, computers, and lights all use electricity.
So do many other appliances that we commonly use.

Key Words

- refrigerator
- appliance
- fossil fuel
- supply
- limit
- conserve
- decrease
- air pollution
- turn off
- air conditioner
- heater

Why is it important to save electricity?
We use fossil fuels, such as coal, oil, and gas, to make electricity.
The supply of fossil fuels is limited.
Once they are gone, they are gone forever.
So we need to conserve them.
This will make the earth's supply of fossil fuels last longer.
It will decrease air pollution as well.

How can we save electricity?
There are many ways to do this.
We can turn off the lights, computers, and TVs
when we are not using them.
We should not keep refrigerators open for a long time.
In the summer, use your air conditioner less often.
In the winter, don't turn the heater up too high.
Take buses and trains or ride a bike when you can.

✔ Ways to Conserve Electricity

Turn off the light when not using it.

Use the air conditioner less often.

Don't keep the refrigerator open for a long time.

Don't turn the heater up too high.

Use public transportation.

Ride a bike.

Main Idea and Details

1   **What is the main idea of the passage?**
   a. We use fossil fuels to make electricity.
   b. We should turn off the lights in empty rooms.
   c. We need to save electricity.

2   **What can you conserve by saving electricity?**
   a. Trees.   **b.** Fossil fuels.   **c.** Batteries.

3   **What does commonly mean?**
   a. Often.   **b.** Rarely.   **c.** Never.

4   **Answer the questions.**
   a. What are some fossil fuels? _____
   b. How can we make the earth's fossil fuel supply last longer? _____
   c. What should we do in the summer? _____

5   **Complete the outline.**

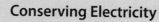

Conserving Electricity

| What Uses Electricity | Fossil Fuels | How to Save Electricity |

What Uses Electricity
- Many ᵃ_____ such as refrigerators, TVs, and computers
- Lights, air conditioners, and heaters

Fossil Fuels
- Coal, oil, and gas
- Have limited ᵇ_____
- Must conserve them

How to Save Electricity
- Turn off lights, computers, and TVs
- Do not keep ᶜ_____ open for a long time
- Use ᵈ_____ and heaters less often
- Take buses or trains or ride a bike

Vocabulary Builder

Write the correct words and the meanings in Chinese.

 **1** ▸ a large container used for keeping food and drinks cold
_____

 **2** ▸ an electrical machine, such as a refrigerator, that is used in the home
_____

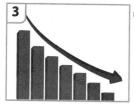 **3** ▸ to make (something) smaller in size, amount, number, etc.
_____

 **4** ▸ to prevent land, water, or other natural resources from being damaged or destroyed
_____

Motion and Forces

Key Words

- curve
- zigzag
- motion
- speed
- force
- push
- pull
- gravity
- friction
- rub

There are many ways things move.

Things can move forward and backward, curve, or zigzag.

When something is moving, it is in motion.

Different objects move at different speeds.

Speed is how fast something moves over a certain distance.

Snails move at very slow speeds.

Airplanes move at very high speeds.

Many things can move with a little force.

A force is a push or a pull that makes an object move.

Forces can change an object's motion and speed.

Gravity is one of these forces.

Gravity is the force that pulls things toward Earth.

Things fall to the ground because they are pulled by Earth's gravity.

Friction occurs when two objects rub against each other.

Friction can slow down or stop objects in motion.

Bike brakes use friction to stop the bike.

✓ Things can move with various forces.

push

pull

You use forces to move things.

Gravity pulls objects toward the ground.

Friction makes something move slower.

Main Idea and Details

1   What is the passage mainly about?
   a. Gravity and friction.
   b. The speeds different things move at.
   c. Motion and the forces that affect motion.

2   Two objects rubbing against each other create _____ .
   a. friction   **b.** gravity   **c.** speed

3   How can different things move?
   a. Only forward.   **b.** Only backward.   **c.** In many directions.

4   Complete the sentences.
   a. Airplanes can move at very fast _____ .
   b. The force that pulls things toward Earth is _____ .
   c. Friction slows _____ or stops moving objects.

5   Complete the outline.

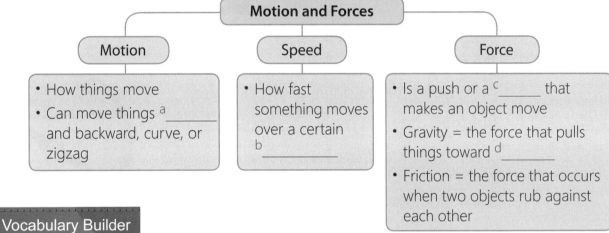

Motion and Forces

Motion
- How things move
- Can move things ᵃ_____ and backward, curve, or zigzag

Speed
- How fast something moves over a certain ᵇ_____

Force
- Is a push or a ᶜ_____ that makes an object move
- Gravity = the force that pulls things toward ᵈ_____
- Friction = the force that occurs when two objects rub against each other

Vocabulary Builder

Write the correct words and the meanings in Chinese.

 **1** ▸ how fast something moves
_____

 **2** ▸ an act or process of moving
_____

 **3** ▸ the force that pulls things toward Earth
_____

 **4** ▸ to move along a path that has a series of short, sharp turns or angles
_____

Magnets

Magnets pull things toward them.

Put some paper clips, rubber bands, or pens on a table.

Bring a magnet near them. Which objects will the magnet pull?

Magnets attract, or pull, things made of iron or steel.

But magnets do not attract things made of plastic, paper, or rubber.

Magnets can also push or pull other magnets.

All magnets have two poles.

The N shows the north-seeking pole.

The S shows the south-seeking pole.

Opposite poles attract each other.

If the N pole of one magnet is near the S pole of another magnet, the poles attract each other.

Like poles repel each other.

If you bring two N poles or two S poles together, they will repel one another.

We use magnets in many ways.

One of the most useful things is a compass.

A magnetized compass needle can show us which direction we are going.

There are magnets in computer discs and televisions.

Credit cards and bank cards also have magnets.

Key Words

- magnet
- attract
- pole
- north-seeking pole = N pole
- south-seeking pole = S pole
- repel
- compass
- magnetized
- compass needle

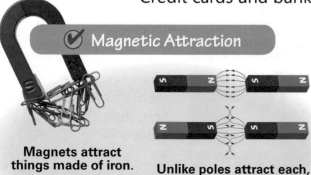

✓ **Magnetic Attraction**

Magnets attract things made of iron.

Unlike poles attract each, but like poles repel other.

✓ **Kinds of Magnets**

round magnet | bar magnet | horseshoe magnet

Magnets come in many shapes and sizes.

Main Idea and Details

1   What is the passage mainly about?
   a. What a compass is.
   b. How magnets work.
   c. What N poles and S poles are.

2   What do magnets attract?
   a. Rubber bands.   **b.** Paper.   **c.** Paper clips.

3   What does repel mean?
   a. Push up.   **b.** Push away.   **c.** Push out.

4   According to the passage, which statement is true?
   a. All magnets have two N poles.
   b. A compass is a kind of magnet.
   c. Magnets can pull iron and rubber.

5   Complete the outline.

Magnets

How They Work

- Pull objects toward them
- Attract things made of ª_____ or steel
- Have two poles: N pole and S pole
- Opposite poles ᵇ_____ each other.
- Like poles repel each other.

Magnets in Objects

- Compass = has a ᶜ_____ needle that shows people which way they are going
- There're magnets in computer discs, televisions, ᵈ_____, and bank cards.

Vocabulary Builder

Write the correct words and the meanings in Chinese.

▸ an object that can pull things made of iron or steel
_____

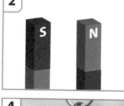
▸ one of the two ends of a magnet
_____

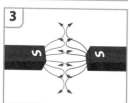
▸ to push away
_____

▸ the magnetized pointer of a compass
_____

Vocabulary | **Review 5**

A Complete the sentences with the words below.

| power | limited | heater | electric machines |
| store | through | electricity | air conditioner |

1   Electricity provides _____ for many things to work.

2   An electric current runs _____ a wire.

3   Electricity moves from outlets, through plugs and wires, into _____
_____.

4   A battery can _____ energy inside it and change the energy to electricity.

5   Refrigerators, TVs, computers, and lights all use _____.

6   The supply of fossil fuels is _____.

7   In the summer, use your _____ _____ less often.

8   In the winter, don't turn the _____ up too high.

B Complete the sentences with the words below.

| motion | magnetized | pull | repel |
| forward | toward | attract | rub |

1   Things can move _____ and backward, curve, or zigzag.

2   When something is moving, it is in _____.

3   A force is a push or a _____ that makes an object move.

4   Gravity is the force that pulls things _____ Earth.

5   Friction occurs when two objects _____ against each other.

6   Magnets _____, or pull, things made of iron or steel.

7   If you bring two N poles or two S poles together, they will _____ one another.

8   A _____ compass needle can show us which direction we are going.

58

C

Write the correct word and the meaning in Chinese.

1 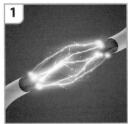 ▸ a flow of electricity

_____

2  ▸ a small electric light that you can carry in your hand

_____

3  ▸ an electrical machine, such as a refrigerator, that is used in the home

_____

4  ▸ the force that pulls things toward Earth

_____

5  ▸ the force that occurs when two objects rub against each other

_____

6  ▸ an object that can pull things made of iron or steel

_____

D

Match each word with the correct definition and write the meaning in Chinese.

1 glow _____ ☐

2 wire _____ ☐

3 appliance _____ ☐

4 fossil fuel _____ ☐

5 air pollution _____ ☐

6 speed _____ ☐

7 force _____ ☐

8 attract _____ ☐

9 repel _____ ☐

10 compass _____ ☐

a. to push away

b. how fast something moves

c. a fuel such as coal and oil

d. to shine with a gentle, steady light

e. the process of polluting the air

f. an instrument that shows directions

g. a push or a pull that makes an object move

h. to pull; to make someone interested in something

i. a string-like piece of metal used to carry an electric current

j. an electrical machine, such as a refrigerator, that is used in the home

What Is Sound?

Key Words

- sound
- vibration
- vibrate
- ring
- speaker
- sound wave
- loud
- speed of sound

Sound is a form of energy that is made by vibrations.
To make sound, you need to make something move.

When you hit a drum, it vibrates and makes sound.
You hear a phone ring because a small speaker inside it vibrates.
All objects make sounds when they vibrate.
When the vibrations stop, the sounds stop.

Sound travels through the air.
When something vibrates, the air around it vibrates, too.
Then, it produces sound waves.
You hear the sound when the sound waves reach your ear.
Sounds can be loud or soft and high or low, but they are all
produced by sound waves.

Sound moves very quickly.
It can move 340 meters per second.
We call this the speed of sound.
Nowadays, many airplanes can fly faster than the speed of sound.

✓ Sound is made by vibrations.

Objects make sounds when they vibrate.

✓ Sound Waves

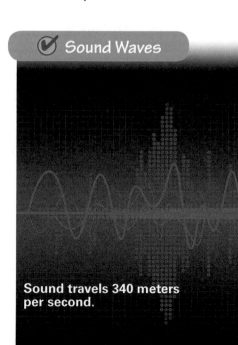

Sound travels 340 meters per second.

Main Idea and Details

1 **What is the passage mainly about?**

    a. How to make different sounds.

    b. How sound is made and moves.

    c. How to hear sounds.

2 **The _____ of sound is 340 meters per second.**

    a. type   **b.** speed   **c.** vibration

3 **What does vibrating air produce?**

    a. Drumming sounds.   **b.** Ringing sounds.   **c.** Sound waves.

4 **Answer the questions.**

    a. What is sound? _____

    b. How does sound travel? _____

    c. What can go faster than the speed of sound? _____

5 **Complete the outline.**

```
                          Sound
         ┌───────────────────────────────────┐
      Vibrations                         Sound Waves
```

Vibrations	Sound Waves
• Are formed when something moves • All objects make sounds when they ^a_____. • Sounds ^b_____ when vibrations stop.	• Travel through the ^c_____ • We can hear sound when sound waves reach our ear. • Can travel at 340 meters per ^d_____

Vocabulary Builder

Write the correct words and the meanings in Chinese.

 **1** ▸ to shake with repeated small, fast movements

_____

 **2** ▸ the waves of energy that we hear as sound

_____

 **3** ▸ to make a sound especially as a signal of something

_____

 **4** ▸ the speed at which sound waves travel

_____

Sounds and Safety

Key Words

- siren
- whisper
- loudness
- whistle
- pitch
- extremely
- warn
- fire alarm
- smoke detector
- ambulance
- emergency

There are different kinds of sounds.

Sounds can be loud or soft and high or low.

A siren makes a loud sound. A whisper is soft.

The loudness of a sound is how loud or soft it is.

A whistle makes a sound with a high pitch.

The pitch of a sound is how high or low it is.

Many people dislike very loud sounds.

Some extremely loud sounds can even hurt people's ears.

But not all loud sounds are bad.

Some sounds warn you about danger.

In fact, some loud sounds can save people's lives.

Fire alarms can produce very loud sounds.

They tell you to move to a safe place.

Smoke detectors are similar to fire alarms.

When there is smoke, they make loud noises.

Ambulances and police cars have loud sirens and flashing lights.

They warn other drivers on the road of an emergency.

✓ Some loud sounds save people's lives.

Fire alarms and smoke
alarms blow sirens.

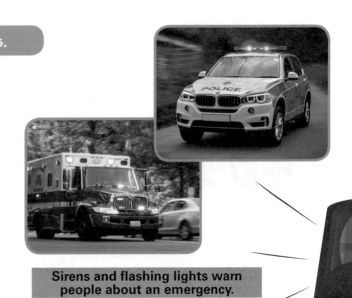

Sirens and flashing lights warn
people about an emergency.

Main Idea and Details

1 **What is the passage mainly about?**
   a. Good but loud sounds.
   b. Fire alarms and smoke detectors.
   c. Many kinds of sounds.

2 **What kind of sound is a whisper?**
   a. A low sound.   **b.** A high sound.   **c.** A soft sound.

3 **What does produce mean?**
   a. Discover.   **b.** Make.   **c.** Invent.

4 **Complete the sentences.**
   a. What kind of sound does a siren make? _____
   b. What can very loud sounds do to people's ears? _____
   c. What have loud sirens and flashing lights? _____

5 **Complete the outline.**

```
                          Sounds
         ┌───────────────┘      └───────────────┐
   Kinds of Sounds                          Loud Sounds
```

- a _____ = loud sound
- Whisper = soft sound
- b _____ = a sound with a high pitch

- Can hurt people's ears
- Fire alarms = tell people to move to a safe place
- Smoke c _____ = make loud noises when there is smoke
- Ambulances and police cars = have loud sirens and flashing lights to warn people about an d _____

Vocabulary Builder

Write the correct words and the meanings in Chinese.

1 ▸ a piece of equipment that makes a loud sound, used for warning people
_____

2 STOP DANGER ▸ to tell someone that something dangerous may happen
_____

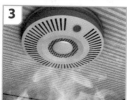
3 ▸ a device that makes a loud and harsh noise when smoke fills a room
_____

4 ▸ a special vehicle for taking sick or injured people to the hospital
_____

The Organs of the Human Body

Key Words

- organ
- unique
- function
- brain
- lung
- circulatory
- nervous
- mental
- respiratory
- stomach
- liver
- intestines
- digest

There are many different organs in your body.

Every organ has its own unique function.

They also work together as parts of the organ systems.

Some of the most important organs are the heart, brain, and lungs.

The heart is part of the circulatory system.

It pumps blood all throughout the body.

The brain runs the body's nervous system.

It sends messages all around your body.

It controls both mental and physical activities.

The lungs are part of the respiratory system.

They enable you to breathe.

The stomach, liver, and intestines help the body digest food.

The stomach breaks food into small pieces.

The liver produces chemicals and sends them to the small intestine to help it further digest food.

The liver also cleans your blood.

The large and small intestines absorb nutrients from food.

✔ The Organ System

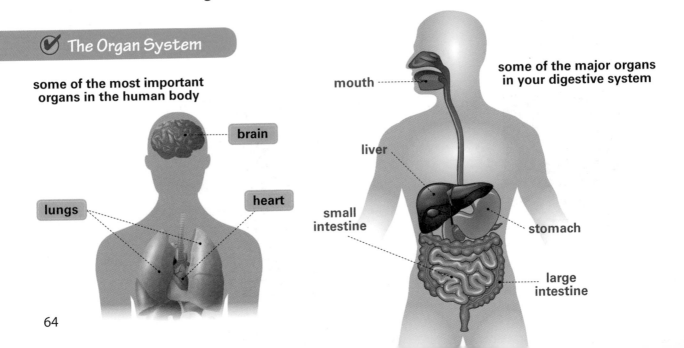

some of the most important organs in the human body

brain

lungs

heart

some of the major organs in your digestive system

mouth

liver

small intestine

stomach

large intestine

Main Idea and Details

1   What is the main idea of the passage?

a. The organs all have important functions.

b. There are many organs in the human body.

c. The heart, brain, and lungs are the most important organs.

2   The _____ helps the body digest food.

a. lungs   b. liver   c. heart

3   What does absorb mean?

a. Clean out.   b. Move around.   c. Soak up.

4   According to the passage, which statement is true?

a. The brain pumps blood to the body.

b. The liver cleans the blood in the body.

c. The small intestines enable people to breathe.

5   Complete the outline.

The Organ System

Heart, Brain, and Lungs
- Are the most important organs
- a _____ = pumps blood throughout the body
- Brain = controls mental and physical activities
- Lungs = enable the body to b _____

Stomach, Liver, and Intestines
- Help the body digest food
- c _____ = breaks food into small pieces
- Liver = helps digest food and cleans the blood
- d _____ = absorb nutrients from food

Vocabulary Builder

Write the correct words and the meanings in Chinese.

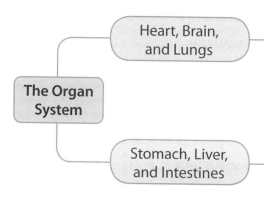

1 ▸ a part of the body such as the heart, brain, or lungs

_____

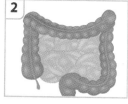

2 ▸ a long tube in the body that helps digest food after it leaves the stomach

_____

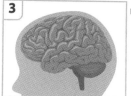

3 ▸ the organ that runs the body's nervous system

_____

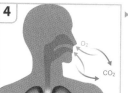

4 ▸ relating to breathing

_____

The Five Senses

You have five senses that help you react to your surroundings.
They are sight, smell, hearing, taste, and touch.
The eyes, nose, ears, tongue, and skin are the sense organs in your body.

Key Words

- sense
- react
- sight
- taste
- touch
- tongue
- sense organ
- optic nerve
- pleasant
- eardrum
- vibrate
- bitter

You use your eyes to see with.
The optic nerves help you see things.
Thanks to sight, you can read books, watch movies, and do other activities.

You use your nose to smell with.
There are all kinds of smells.
Some are pleasant while others are not so nice.

Your ears let you hear the things around you.
Sounds travel through the air in waves.
When some of those sound waves enter your ears and make your eardrums vibrate, you hear the sound.

Your tongue helps you taste things you eat and drink.
Sweet, sour, bitter, and salty are the main four tastes.

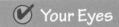

Your skin gives you your sense of touch.
You can feel things physically, especially through your sense of touch.

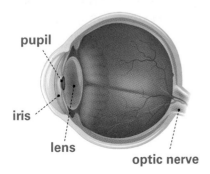

✓ Your Eyes

pupil

iris

lens

optic nerve

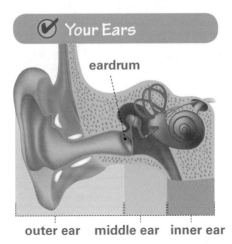

✓ Your Ears

eardrum

outer ear   middle ear   inner ear

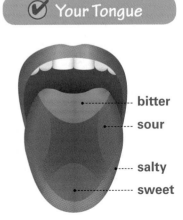

✓ Your Tongue

bitter

sour

salty

sweet

Main Idea and Details

1 **What is the passage mainly about?**

   a. How the body works.

   b. The best of the senses.

   c. The five senses of the body.

2 **What helps people taste things?**

   a. The skin.   **b.** The ears.   **c.** The tongue.

3 **What does react mean?**

   a. Retell.   **b.** Respond.   **c.** Refer.

4 **Complete the sentences.**

   a. Optic nerves let people _____.

   b. A person _____ with his or her nose.

   c. The skin lets a person have a sense of _____.

5 **Complete the outline.**

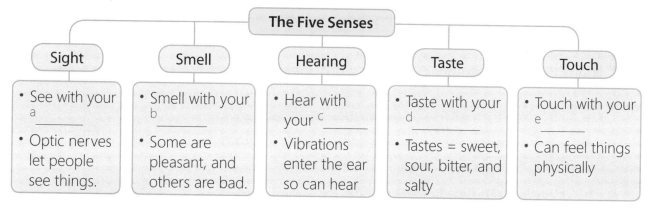

The Five Senses

Sight	Smell	Hearing	Taste	Touch
• See with your a _____	• Smell with your b _____	• Hear with your c _____	• Taste with your d _____	• Touch with your e _____
• Optic nerves let people see things.	• Some are pleasant, and others are bad.	• Vibrations enter the ear so can hear	• Tastes = sweet, sour, bitter, and salty	• Can feel things physically

Vocabulary Builder

Write the correct words and the meanings in Chinese.

 **1** ▸ the organs such as the eyes, nose, and ears

_____

 **2** ▸ the clear part of the eye that focuses light to form clear images

_____

 **3** ▸ having a strong and often unpleasant flavor that is the opposite of sweet

_____

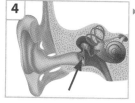 **4** ▸ the part inside your ear which vibrates when sound waves reach it

_____

Vocabulary **Review 6**

A Complete the sentences with the words below.

vibrate	pitch	energy	ambulances
loud	warns	hurt	speed of sound

1   Sound is a form of _____ that is made by vibrations.

2   All objects make sounds when they _____.

3   Sounds can be _____ or soft and high or low, but they are all produced by sound waves.

4   Nowadays, many airplanes can fly faster than the _____ ____ _____.

5   A whistle makes a sound with a high _____.

6   Some extremely loud sounds can even _____ people's ears.

7   Some sound _____ you about danger.

8   _____ and police cars have loud sirens and flashing lights.

B Complete the sentences with the words below.

circulatory	tongue	react	sight
intestines	function	brain	physically

1   Every organ has its own unique _____.

2   The heart is part of the _____ system.

3   The _____ runs the body's nervous system.

4   The stomach, liver, and _____ help the body digest food.

5   You have five senses that help you _____ to your surroundings.

6   Thanks to _____, you can read books, watch movies, and do other activities.

7   Your _____ helps you taste things you eat and drink.

8   You can feel things _____, especially through your sense of touch.

C

Write the correct word and the meaning in Chinese.

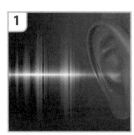 **1**
▸ the waves of energy that we hear as sound

_____

 **2**
▸ a thing that makes a loud noise to warn people about a fire in a building

_____

 **3**
▸ a piece of equipment that makes a loud sound, used for warning people

_____

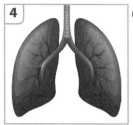 **4**
▸ one of the two organs in your chest that fill with air when you breathe

_____

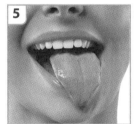 **5**
▸ the soft part in your mouth that is used for tasting and speaking

_____

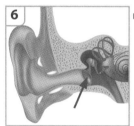 **6**
▸ the part inside your ear which vibrates when sound waves reach it

_____

D

Match each word with the correct definition and write the meaning in Chinese.

1 vibrate _____ ☐

2 loud _____ ☐

3 speed of sound _____ ☐

4 whisper _____ ☐

5 warn _____ ☐

6 nervous _____ ☐

7 stomach _____ ☐

8 respiratory _____ ☐

9 sense organs _____ ☐

10 optic nerve _____ ☐

a. relating to breathing

b. making a lot of noise; not quiet

c. relating to the nerves in your body

d. a nerve that helps you see things

e. the speed at which sound waves travel

f. the organs such as the eyes, nose, and ears

g. the organ that breaks food down into small pieces

h. to shake with repeated small, fast movements

i. to tell someone that something dangerous may happen

j. a very soft and quiet voice; to say something very quietly

A Write the correct word for each sentence.

mantle	vibrations	occurs	crust	phases
launched	electricity	Earth	organs	force

1 The _____ is the thin outermost layer of the earth.

2 The _____ is the earth's thickest layer and is full of hot melted rock.

3 The different moon shapes are called the _____ of the moon.

4 On July 16, *Apollo 11* was _____ from the Kennedy Space Center.

5 _____ provides power for many things to work.

6 A _____ is a push or a pull that makes an object move.

7 Friction _____ when two objects rub against each other.

8 Gravity is the force that pulls things toward _____.

9 Sound is a form of energy that is made by _____.

10 Some of the most important _____ are the heart, brain, and lungs.

B Write the meanings of the words in Chinese.

1	crust	_____	16	speed	_____
2	inner core	_____	17	force	_____
3	lava	_____	18	gravity	_____
4	satellite	_____	19	attract	_____
5	astronaut	_____	20	repel	_____
6	outermost	_____	21	sound wave	_____
7	violent	_____	22	organ	_____
8	appearance	_____	23	tongue	_____
9	reflect	_____	24	eardrum	_____
10	launch	_____	25	vibrate	_____
11	glow	_____	26	whisper	_____
12	wire	_____	27	nervous	_____
13	appliance	_____	28	stomach	_____
14	fossil fuel	_____	29	optic nerve	_____
15	air pollution	_____	30	sense organs	_____

3

- **Mathematics**
- **Language**
- **Visual Arts**
- **Music**

Word Problems

As you practice math, you will do many word problems. When you solve a word problem, you need to figure out what the word problem is asking you to do.

What is this word problem asking you to do?

> There are five beetles on a leaf. Soon, seven more beetles join them. How many beetles are there in all?

This is an addition problem.
To solve it, you can write a number sentence like this: $5 + 7 = 12$.
Number sentences replace words with numbers.
The numbers you add, 5 and 7, are called the addends.
The answer you get, 12, is called the sum.

Now try another word problem.

> Kevin brings ten cookies to the picnic. He eats four of them. How many cookies are left now?

This is a subtraction problem.
To solve it, you can write a number sentence like this: $10 - 4 = 6$.
The number left over, 6, is called the difference.

The signs in a number sentence, such as *+ (plus)*, *− (minus)*, and *= (equals)*, are called the operation signs.

Key Words

• word problem
• solve
• figure out
• addition
• number sentence
• replace
• addend
• sum
• subtraction
• difference
• operation sign

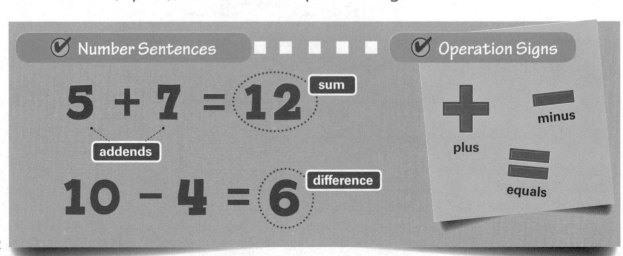

☑ **Number Sentences**

$$5 + 7 = 12 \text{ sum}$$

addends

$$10 - 4 = 6 \text{ difference}$$

☑ **Operation Signs**

+ plus
− minus
= equals

Main Idea and Details

1   What is the main idea of the passage?

a. The numbers you add are called the addends.

b. The signs in a number sentence are operation signs.

c. You can make number sentences to solve word problems.

2   The answer to a subtraction problem is called the _____.

a. difference   b. addend   c. sum

3   What are +, −, and = called?

a. Number sentences.   b. Operation signs.   c. Expressions.

4   Complete the sentences.

a. The answer to an _____ problem is called the sum.

b. 10 _____ 4 equals 6.

c. To solve a word problem, you need to _____ _____ what the problem is asking you to do.

5   Complete the outline.

Word Problems and Number Sentences

Word Problems

- To solve a word problem, figure out what the ᵃ_____ is asking you to do.
- Write a number sentence to add or to ᵇ_____.

Number Sentences

- Replace words with numbers.
- The numbers being added are the ᶜ_____.
- The total is the sum.
- The number left over after subtracting is the ᵈ_____.
- +, −, and = are operation signs.

Vocabulary Builder

Write the correct words and the meanings in Chinese.

1

▸ to understand; to solve

_____

2

Kevin brings ten cookies to the picnic. He eats four of them. How many cookies are left now?

▸ a mathematical problem expressed entirely in words

_____

3

▸ the numbers being added in an addition problem

_____

4

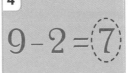

▸ the number that remains after subtraction

_____

Place Value

Key Words

- digit
- value
- one-digit number
- put together
- two-digit number
- three-digit number
- place value
- determine
- location

In math, there are ten digits.

They are 0, 1, 2, 3, 4, 5, 6, 7, 8, and 9.

Each digit has a certain value.

A number from 0 to 9 is a one-digit number.

But we can put two digits together to make a two-digit number.

For example, 10 is a number with two digits.

A two-digit number has a value from 10 to 99.

A three-digit number has three digits together.

For example, 100 is a number with three digits.

A three-digit number has a value from 100 to 999.

We know the value of each digit because of place value.

The value of each number is determined by its location.

Look at the number 245.

The 2 is in the hundreds place, so its value is 200.

The 4 is in the tens place, so its value is 40.

The 5 is in the ones place, so its value is 5.

In other words, 245 means that it has 2 hundreds, 4 tens, and 5 ones.

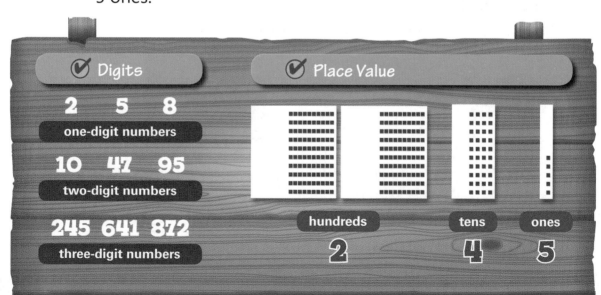

Digits

2 5 8
one-digit numbers

10 47 95
two-digit numbers

245 641 872
three-digit numbers

Place Value

hundreds   tens   ones
2   4   5

Main Idea and Details

1 **What is the passage mainly about?**

   a. Digits and their place values.

   b. Three-digit numbers.

   c. The numbers from 0 to 9.

2 **How many digits are in 42?**

   a. One.   **b.** Two.   **c.** Three.

3 **What does location mean?**

   a. Place.   **b.** Digit.   **c.** Value.

4 **According to the passage, which statement is true?**

   a. All of the numbers from 0 to 9 have one digit.

   b. A three-digit number is 99 or less.

   c. In 342, the 4 is in the hundreds place.

5 **Complete the outline.**

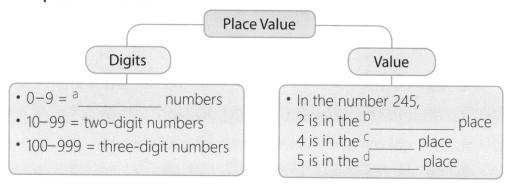

Place Value

Digits
- 0–9 = ª _____ numbers
- 10–99 = two-digit numbers
- 100–999 = three-digit numbers

Value
- In the number 245,
  2 is in the ᵇ_____ place
  4 is in the ᶜ_____ place
  5 is in the ᵈ_____ place

Vocabulary Builder

Write the correct words and the meanings in Chinese.

1  ▸ any of the single numbers from 0 to 9

_____

2  ▸ the value of the position of a digit in a number

_____

3  ▸ any number that has a value from 10 to 99

_____

4  ▸ any number that has a value from 100 to 999

_____

Multiplication and Division

Key Words

- multiplication
- multiply
- equal group
- multiple times
- factor
- product
- division
- separate
- dividend
- divide
- divisor
- quotient

Imagine you have 5 groups of oranges with 3 oranges each.

How many oranges do you have?

You could add them together like this: 3+3+3+3+3=15.

Or, you could use multiplication. 5×3=15.

→ 5×3=15

When you multiply, you add equal groups of numbers multiple times.

It is a quick way of adding the same number over and over again.

When you multiply, the numbers that are being multiplied are the factors.

And the answer is the product.

Now, imagine you have 20 apples.

You want to make them 4 groups with the same number of apples.

You can find the answer by using division. 20÷4=5.

You can make 4 groups that have 5 apples each.

→ 20÷4=5

Division separates a number into equal groups.

The dividend is the big number being divided.

The divisor is the number doing the dividing.

And the quotient is the answer.

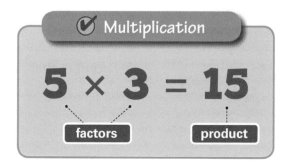

✓ Multiplication

5 × 3 = 15

factors   product

✓ Division

20 ÷ 4 = 5

dividend   divisor   quotient

1 **What is the passage mainly about?**

   a. Factors and products.

   b. Multiplying and dividing.

   c. Dividends and quotients.

2 **The answer to a multiplication problem is the** _____.

   a. product   **b.** factor   **c.** multiple

3 **What is the big number being divided called?**

   a. The quotient.   **b.** The divisor.   **c.** The dividend.

4 **Answer the questions.**

   a. What is multiplication? _____

   b. What are the numbers being multiplied called? _____

   c. What is division? _____

5 **Complete the outline.**

Operations

Multiplication

- Is adding equal groups of numbers
  a _____ _____
- Numbers being multiplied = factors
- The answer = b _____

Division

- Is separating a number into
  c _____ _____
- d _____ = the big number being divided
- Divisor = the number doing the dividing
- Quotient = the answer

Write the correct words and the meanings in Chinese.

1	▸ the numbers that are being multiplied

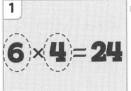

_____

2	▸ to add equal groups of numbers multiple times

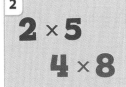

_____

3	▸ the big number being divided

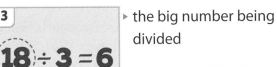

_____

4	▸ the answer to a division problem

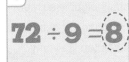

_____

Skip Counting Equal Groups

Key Words

- count
- skip count
- by twos/fives/ tens
- omit
- backward
- multiplication table

Sometimes, we want to count quickly.

Counting one by one can be very slow.

But, if we skip count, we can count much faster.

Let's count to ten: 1, 2, 3, 4, 5, 6, 7, 8, 9, 10.

Now let's skip count to ten by twos: 2, 4, 6, 8, 10.

Skip counting by twos was two times faster than using every number.

Now, let's skip count by fives: 5, 10, 15, 20, 25, 30, 35, 40, 45, 50.

And let's skip count by tens: 10, 20, 30, 40, 50, 60, 70, 80, 90, 100.

Every time we skip count, we can omit other numbers.

This lets us count to big numbers very quickly.

We can even skip count backward.

Skip count backward by twos: 10, 8, 6, 4, 2, 0.

What's the easiest way to learn skip counting?

It is to learn the multiplication tables.

They teach you how to skip count by many different numbers.

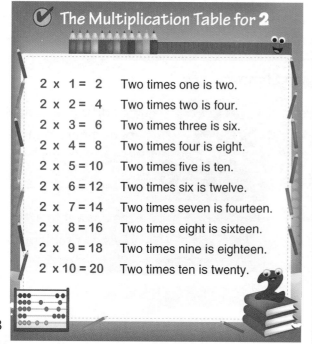

The Multiplication Table for 2

2 x 1 = 2	Two times one is two.
2 x 2 = 4	Two times two is four.
2 x 3 = 6	Two times three is six.
2 x 4 = 8	Two times four is eight.
2 x 5 = 10	Two times five is ten.
2 x 6 = 12	Two times six is twelve.
2 x 7 = 14	Two times seven is fourteen.
2 x 8 = 16	Two times eight is sixteen.
2 x 9 = 18	Two times nine is eighteen.
2 x 10 = 20	Two times ten is twenty.

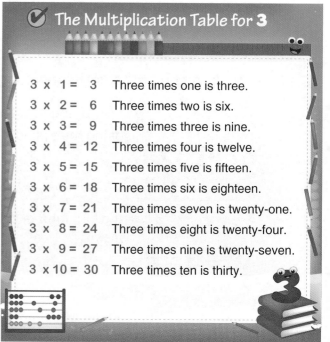

The Multiplication Table for 3

3 x 1 = 3	Three times one is three.
3 x 2 = 6	Three times two is six.
3 x 3 = 9	Three times three is nine.
3 x 4 = 12	Three times four is twelve.
3 x 5 = 15	Three times five is fifteen.
3 x 6 = 18	Three times six is eighteen.
3 x 7 = 21	Three times seven is twenty-one.
3 x 8 = 24	Three times eight is twenty-four.
3 x 9 = 27	Three times nine is twenty-seven.
3 x 10 = 30	Three times ten is thirty.

Main Idea and Details

1 **What is the passage mainly about?**

a. Counting backward.

b. Multiplication tables.

c. Skip counting.

2 **How can we skip count by twos?**

a. 5, 10, 15, 20, 25, 30.   b. 10, 20, 30, 40, 50, 60.   c. 2, 4, 6, 8, 10.

3 **What does omit mean?**

a. Leave out.   b. Leave around.   c. Leave with.

4 **Complete the sentences.**

a. Skip counting lets you count _____ than counting one by one.

b. You omit _____ when you skip count.

c. The _____ tables teach you how to skip count.

5 **Complete the outline.**

Skip Counting

Why People Do It

• Can ᵃ_____ faster than counting one by one
• Lets you omit numbers
• Can count to big numbers ᵇ_____

Multiplication Tables

• Teach you ᶜ_____ _____ skip count by various numbers
• Is the best way to learn skip counting

Vocabulary Builder

Write the correct words and the meanings in Chinese.

1

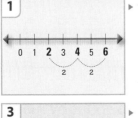

▶ to count forwards or backwards by a number other than 1

_____

2

2, 3̶, 4, 5̶, 6, 7̶, 8, 9̶

▶ to leave out; not to include something

_____

3

10, 9, 8 …

9, 6, 3 …

▶ toward the back; in the reverse of the usual way

_____

4

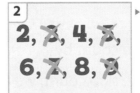

▶ a table that lists the products of certain numbers multiplied together

_____

A

Complete the sentences with the words below.

two-digit	word problem	sentences	digit
hundreds	place value	determined	left

1 When you solve a _____ _____, you need to figure out what the word problem is asking you to do.

2 Number _____ replace words with numbers.

3 In 10−4=6, the number _____ over, 6, is called the difference.

4 Each _____ has a certain value.

5 We know the value of each digit because of _____ _____.

6 The value of each number is _____ by its location.

7 A _____ number has a value from 10 to 99.

8 245 means that it has 2 _____, 4 tens, and 5 ones.

B

Complete the sentences with the words below.

equal groups	multiplied	omit	skip counting
multiple times	divided	fives	multiplication

1 When you multiply, you add equal groups of numbers _____ _____.

2 The numbers that are being _____ are the factors.

3 Division separates a number into _____ _____.

4 The dividend is the big number being _____.

5 _____ _____ by twos was two times faster than using every number.

6 Now, let's skip count by _____: 5, 10, 15, 20, 25, 30, 35, 40, 45, 50.

7 Every time we skip count, we can _____ other numbers.

8 The _____ tables teach you how to skip count by many different numbers.

C

Write the correct word and the meaning in Chinese.

1  ▸ the numbers being added in an addition problem

_____

2 ▸ a sign in a number sentence, such as + or –

_____

3  ▸ any of the single numbers from 0 to 9

_____

4 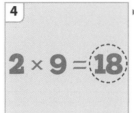 ▸ the answer to a multiplication problem

_____

5 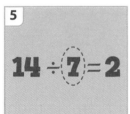 ▸ the number doing the dividing

_____

6 ▸ a table that lists the products of certain numbers multiplied together

_____

D

Match each word with the correct definition and write the meaning in Chinese.

1 figure out _____ ☐

2 replace _____ ☐

3 put together _____ ☐

4 two-digit number _____ ☐

5 three-digit number _____ ☐

6 multiple times _____ ☐

7 skip count _____ ☐

8 divisor _____ ☐

9 omit _____ ☐

10 backward _____ ☐

a. many times

b. to understand; to solve

c. to combine; to join together

d. the number doing the dividing

e. to count forwards or backwards by a number other than 1

f. to leave out; not to include something

g. to take or fill the place of something

h. any number that has a value from 10 to 99

i. any number that has a value from 100 to 999

j. toward the back; in the reverse of the usual way

81

What Are Myths?

Key Words

- myth
  (= mythology)
- mysterious
- experience
- make up
- goddess
- brave
- hero
- terrible
- monster
- ancient
- Greek and
  Roman
  mythology

Myths are stories that have been around for thousands of years or more.

A long time ago, people thought the world was very mysterious. They did not understand many of the things they saw and experienced.

So they often made up stories.

These stories explained the world they lived in.

Today, we call these stories myths.

People all around the world have myths.

Many myths are similar.

They often have gods and goddesses in them.

Some myths are stories about brave heroes and terrible monsters.

Some myths explain things like how the world began, why we have different seasons, or what happens to people after they die. Although we do not believe these stories, we still enjoy them because they are so wonderful.

Some of the most famous myths come to us from ancient Greece and Rome. We call them Greek and Roman mythology.

Myths tell about gods and goddesses, heroes, and monsters.

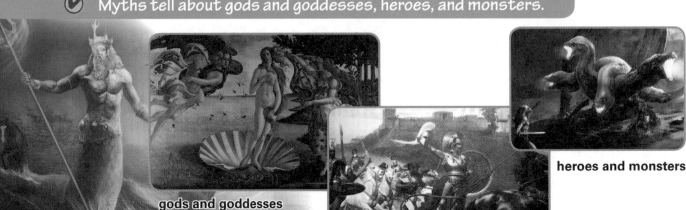

gods and goddesses

heroes and monsters

Main Idea and Details

1 What is the passage mainly about?

a. What myths are.   **b.** Where myths are from.

c. Who told myths.

2 The heroes in many myths are _____.

a. mysterious   **b.** terrible   **c.** brave

3 Where do many famous myths come from?

a. Japan.   **b.** Greece.   **c.** England.

4 According to the passage, which statement is true?

a. Myths always have terrible monsters in them.

b. Myths explained the world ancient people lived in.

c. Myths are new stories that people like to make.

5 Complete the outline.

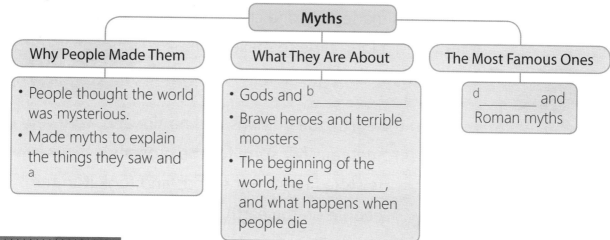

Myths

Why People Made Them

- People thought the world was mysterious.
- Made myths to explain the things they saw and a _____

What They Are About

- Gods and b _____
- Brave heroes and terrible monsters
- The beginning of the world, the c _____, and what happens when people die

The Most Famous Ones

d _____ and Roman myths

Vocabulary Builder

Write the correct words and the meanings in Chinese.

1 ▸ strange and difficult to understand

_____

2 ▸ feeling or showing no fear

_____

3 ▸ a large imaginary creature that looks very ugly and frightening

_____

4 ▸ a story that is believed by many people but that is not true

_____

Prometheus Brings Fire

 Here is a Greek myth about how humans got fire.

Key Words

• Titan
• creature
• gift
• remain
• feel sorry for
• steal
• find out
• furious
• punish
• chain
• fly down
• set free

Once, only giant Titans and gods lived on the earth.
Prometheus was one of the Titans.
One day, Zeus, the king of the gods,
spoke with Prometheus and his brother
Epimetheus.
Zeus ordered them to make some new
creatures.
Epimetheus made many animals.
He gave these animals some gifts.
Prometheus made only one creature: man.
 It took him a long time to make man.
   So there were no gifts remaining for men.

On the earth, the humans had no fire and were very cold.
   Prometheus felt sorry for the humans.
      He stole fire from the gods and took it to the
      people on the earth.
      When Zeus found out what Prometheus had done,
      he was furious.
      To punish him, Zeus chained him to a big rock.
      Every day, an eagle flew down and ate his liver.
      Years later, Prometheus was finally set free by
      Heracles, a great hero.

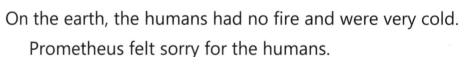

Main Idea and Details

1 What is the passage mainly about?

   a. Why was Zeus upset with Prometheus?

   b. How did Prometheus give fire to man?

   c. Where did Prometheus be punished?

2 What did Prometheus's brother do?

   a. He made an eagle.   **b.** He gave gifts to many animals.

   c. He became the king of the gods.

3 What does furious mean?

   a. Very surprised.   **b.** Very pleased.   **c.** Very angry.

4 Answer the questions.

   a. Who was the king of the gods? _____

   b. Why did Prometheus give fire to humans? _____

   c. Who did free Prometheus from the rock? _____

5 Complete the outline.

Prometheus

Making Man

- Zeus ordered Prometheus and his brother Epimetheus to make creatures.
- Epimetheus made many ᵃ_____.
- Prometheus only made ᵇ_____.

Bringing Fire

- Men were cold.
- Prometheus felt sorry for them.
- Prometheus brought them ᶜ_____.
- Zeus got angry and ᵈ_____ Prometheus to a rock.

Vocabulary Builder

Write the correct words and the meanings in Chinese.

1 ▸ one of a family of giants in Greek mythology

_____

2 ▸ to make someone suffer because he has done something wrong

_____

3 ▸ an animal of any type

_____

4 ▸ to give freedom; to relieve

_____

A noun is a part of speech like a verb or an adjective.

A noun names a person, place, or thing.

John, *city*, and *book* are all nouns.

Key Words

- noun
- part of speech
- verb
- adjective
- common noun
- proper noun
- capital letter
- small letter
- singular
- plural

All nouns are common nouns or proper nouns.

A common noun names any person, place, or thing.

Girl, *school*, and *pencil* are common nouns.

A proper noun names a particular person, place, or thing.

Julie, *Mount Everest*, and *Central Elementary School* are proper nouns.

Proper nouns begin with capital letters.

And we use small letters for common nouns.

All nouns are either singular or plural.

A singular noun means there is just one of it.

A plural noun means there are two or more of it.

We often make plural nouns by adding -s, -es, or -ies to singular nouns.

Boy, *watch*, and *story* are singular nouns.

Boys, *watches*, and *stories* are plural nouns.

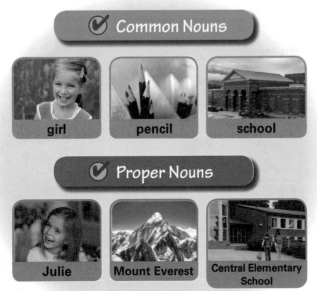

Common Nouns

girl   pencil   school

Proper Nouns

Julie   Mount Everest   Central Elementary School

Singular Nouns

boy   watch   story

Plural Nouns

boys   watches   stories

Main Idea and Details

1 **What is the main idea of the passage?**

a. A noun is a part of speech.

b. There are many kinds of nouns.

c. We use nouns, verbs, and adjectives.

2 _____ **nouns begin with capital letters.**

a. Proper   b. Common   c. Singular

3 **Which word is a singular noun?**

a. Boys.   b. Watches.   c. Story.

4 **Complete the sentences.**

a. A noun is a _____, place, or thing.

b. Common nouns begin with a _____ letter.

c. All nouns are either singular or _____.

5 **Complete the outline.**

Nouns

Common and Proper

- Name a person, place, or thing
- Common noun = ª_____ person, place, or thing
- Proper noun = the name of a ᵇ_____ person, place, or thing

Singular and Plural

- ᶜ_____ noun = just one of it
- Plural noun = two or more of it
- Add -s, -es, or ᵈ_____ to make plural nouns.

Vocabulary Builder

Write the correct words and the meanings in Chinese.

1 noun verb adjective
▸ a class of words such as adjectives, adverbs, nouns, verbs, etc.
_____

2 Jack, Korea, Sunday, Mrs. Brown
▸ It names a particular person, place, or thing.
_____

3 toy, glass, city, room
▸ It names any person, place, or thing.
_____

4 toys, glasses, cities, rooms
▸ It names more than one person, place, or thing.
_____

87

Some Common Sayings

Key Words

- **common saying**
- **proverb**
- **pass on**
- **moral message**
- **wisdom**
- **pass down**
- **oral tradition**
- **well-known**
- **familiar**
- **advise**
- **patient**

Every culture has common sayings or proverbs.

Common sayings or proverbs often have special meanings.

They pass on moral messages.

Or they have some wisdom that people can learn from.

Many sayings or proverbs are passed down from the oral tradition.

English has many common sayings.

"There's no place like home" is a well-known saying.

People use this saying to mean that travel may be pleasant, but home is the best place of all.

"Rome wasn't built in a day" is another familiar saying.

This saying advises us to be patient.

We cannot do great things quickly.

So we should take our time and be patient.

"Practice makes perfect" is a common saying, too.

This saying tells us to keep trying.

When we try something new, we are usually not good at it.

But, by practicing, we can become perfect at it.

 Some Well-known Common Sayings

There's no place like home.

Rome wasn't built in a day.

Practice makes perfect.

Main Idea and Details

1   What is the passage mainly about?

a. Different cultures.

b. A famous proverb.

c. Some common sayings.

2   Where do many sayings and proverbs come from?

a. The oral tradition.   b. Books.   c. Television shows.

3   What does familiar mean?

a. Old.   b. Well-known.   c. Original.

4   According to the passage, which statement is true?

a. All sayings and proverbs are the same.

b. It took one day to build Rome.

c. Some sayings pass on moral messages.

5   Complete the outline.

Common Sayings and Proverbs

Features

- Have special meanings
- Pass on moral ª _____
- Have wisdom to learn
- Come from the ᵇ_____ tradition

Famous Sayings and Proverbs

- There's no place like home.
- Rome wasn't ᶜ_____ in a day.
- ᵈ_____ makes perfect.

Vocabulary Builder

Write the correct words and the meanings in Chinese.

 Time is money.
▸ a saying that gives a moral message or advice about life

_____

▸ knowledge of what is proper or reasonable

_____

▸ a tradition passed down by word of mouth from one generation to another

_____

▸ to give (something) to a younger person

_____

A Complete the sentences with the words below.

| how | myths | heroes | ancient |
| stole | titans | punish | creature |

1 _____ are stories that have been around for thousands of years or more.

2 Some myths are stories about brave _____ and terrible monsters.

3 Some myths explain things like _____ the world began or why we have different seasons.

4 Some of the most famous myths come to us from _____ Greece and Rome.

5 Once, only giant _____ and gods lived on the earth.

6 Prometheus made only one _____: man.

7 Prometheus _____ fire from the gods and took it to the people on Earth.

8 To _____ Prometheus, Zeus chained him to a big rock.

B Complete the sentences with the words below.

| capital | part of speech | sayings | perfect |
| adding | common noun | familiar | passed down |

1 A noun is a _____ _____ _____ like a verb or an adjective.

2 A _____ _____ names any person, place, or thing.

3 Proper nouns begin with _____ letters.

4 We often make plural nouns by _____ -s, -es, or -ies to singular nouns.

5 Common _____ or proverbs often have special meanings.

6 Many sayings or proverbs are _____ _____ from the oral tradition.

7 "Rome wasn't built in a day" is a _____ saying.

8 "Practice makes _____" is a common saying.

C **Write the correct word and the meaning in Chinese.**

1 ▸ a female spirit or being that is believed to control the world

_____

2 ▸ a person who is admired for great or brave acts or fine qualities

_____

3 ▸ to make someone suffer because he has done something wrong

_____

4 Jack, Korea, Sunday, Mrs. Brown ▸ It names a particular person, place, or thing.

_____

5 toys, glasses, cities, rooms ▸ It names more than one person, place, or thing.

_____

6 Time is money. ▸ a saying that gives a moral message or advice about life

_____

D **Match each word with the correct definition and write the meaning in Chinese.**

1 mysterious _____ ☐

2 ancient _____ ☐

3 feel sorry for _____ ☐

4 punish _____ ☐

5 set free _____ ☐

6 common noun _____ ☐

7 singular noun _____ ☐

8 pass down _____ ☐

9 oral tradition _____ ☐

10 patient _____ ☐

a. to pass on; to transmit

b. to give freedom; to relieve

c. to feel pity for; to sympathize with

d. It names any person, place, or thing.

e. strange and difficult to understand

f. It names one person, place, or thing.

g. belonging to the distant past; very old

h. bearing or enduring without complaint

i. to make someone suffer because he has done something wrong

j. a tradition passed down by word of mouth from one generation to another

Realistic Art and Abstract Art

Key Words

- artist
- divide
- separate
- realistic art
- abstract art
- reality
- landscape
- Dutch
- unusual
- Spanish

Artists paint many kinds of pictures.

But we can divide all art into two separate groups: realistic art and abstract art.

Realistic art shows objects as they look in reality.

In realistic art, the landscape would look exactly like it does in reality.

So the trees, mountains, and rivers would look real.

Rembrandt, a Dutch artist, was a famous realistic artist.

Abstract art shows objects different from how they look in reality.

Abstract paintings create images in new and unusual ways.

For example, abstract landscapes would not look exactly as they do in reality.

The trees might be green balls.

The mountains might be brown triangles.

And the rivers might be blue lines.

They would not look like real trees, mountains, and rivers at all.

✓ Realistic Art and Abstract Art

 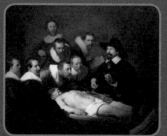  

Rembrandt's realistic works

abstract works

Main Idea and Details

1 **What is the main idea of the passage?**

   a. All art is either realistic or abstract.

   b. Rembrandt and Picasso were two famous painters.

   c. Abstract art shows objects different from their real appearance.

2 **Art can be divided into realistic or _____ art.**

   a. abstract   **b.** landscape   **c.** triangle

3 **What might a mountain look like in abstract art?**

   a. A blue line.   **b.** A green ball.   **c.** A brown triangle.

4 **Answer the questions.**

   a. How would a landscape look in realistic art? _____

   b. Who was a famous realistic painter? _____

   c. What kind of artist was Picasso? _____

5 **Complete the outline.**

Kinds of Art

Realistic Art

- Shows objects as they look in ᵃ_____
- Trees, mountains, and rivers in landscapes look real.
- ᵇ_____ = famous realistic artist

Abstract Art

- Shows objects different from how they look in reality
- ᶜ_____ = green balls
- Mountains = brown triangles
- Rivers = blue lines
- ᵈ_____ = famous abstract artist

Vocabulary Builder

Write the correct words and the meanings in Chinese.

 **1** ▸ someone who makes paintings, sculptures, etc.

_____

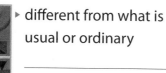 **2** ▸ a picture that shows a natural scene of land; an area of land that has a particular appearance

_____

 **3** ▸ different from what is usual or ordinary

_____

 **4** ▸ art that shows objects in a new and unusual way

_____

Key Words

• Spaniard
• style
• cubism
• geometrical shape
• sculptor
• printmaker
• draw
• sketch
• antiwar
• artwork

There have been many great artists.
One of the greatest was Pablo Picasso.
Picasso was a Spaniard who painted during the twentieth century.

Picasso used many different styles in his paintings.
One of his most famous styles was cubism.
He painted objects in different geometrical shapes.
So he used squares, rectangles, and triangles in his paintings.

Picasso was not just a painter.
He was also a sculptor and printmaker.
He even drew many sketches.
He was interested in all different kinds of art.

One of his most famous paintings was called *Guernica*.
It was a huge painting.
He made it to show his antiwar feelings.

During his life, Picasso made thousands of artworks.
Today, people spend millions of dollars buying
his paintings and other works.

 Cubism Artworks

Main Idea and Details

1 **What is the passage mainly about?**
  a. Picasso's early life.
  b. The art Picasso created.
  c. Picasso's work *Guernica*.

2 **What was a famous style that Picasso used?**
  a. *Guernica*.   b. Cubism.   c. Sculpture.

3 **What does sketches mean?**
  a. Posters.   b. Paintings.   c. Drawings.

4 **Complete the sentences.**
  a. Picasso painted during the _____ century.
  b. Picasso was a painter, _____, and printmaker.
  c. *Guernica* shows the _____ feelings of Picasso.

5 **Complete the outline.**

Picasso

Painting
- Was an abstract artist
- a _____ was his famous style.
- Painted the famous *Guernica*
- b _____ showed his antiwar feelings

Other Art
- Was a sculptor
- Was a c _____
- Drew many sketches
- Made thousands of d _____ in his life

Vocabulary Builder

Write the correct words and the meanings in Chinese.

1 ▸ an artistic movement that featured surfaces of geometrical planes
_____

2 ▸ an artist who makes sculptures
_____

3 ▸ a print artist
_____

4 ▸ a drawing made quickly that does not have many details
_____

Many Kinds of Music

Key Words

- classical music
- musical instrument
- orchestra
- symphony
- concerto
- soloist
- opera
- choral music
- folk song
- patriotic music
- national anthem

There are many different kinds of music.
One of them is classical music.
Classical music relies mostly on musical instruments.
The piano, violin, cello, and flute are some
popular classical music instruments.

There are many forms of classical music, too.
A long piece of music played by an orchestra
is called a symphony.
A concerto is for an orchestra, too.
But it has some parts for soloists to play.
Operas and choral music are two other forms
of music that involve singing.

Folk songs are songs that have been passed down for many years.
Every country has its own folk music.
It is usually fun to listen to.
Most traditional music is folk music.

Patriotic music is songs and music like national anthems.
Patriotic music makes people feel proud of their country.

Kinds of Music

classical music

folk music

patriotic music

choral music

Main Idea and Details

1 **What is the main idea of the passage?**

a. Concertos and operas are forms of classical music.

b. There are a lot of different kinds of music.

c. National anthems are a kind of patriotic music.

2 **Folk music is often** _____ **music.**

a. traditional   b. patriotic   c. choral

3 **How do people feel when they listen to patriotic music?**

a. Proud of their country.   b. Fun about their country.

c. Upset about their country.

4 **According to the passage, which statement is true?**

a. Only the soloist plays in a concerto.

b. The piano and violin are used in classical music.

c. Folk music is usually very patriotic.

5 **Complete the outline.**

```
                         Kinds of Music
          ┌──────────────────┼──────────────────┐
   Classical Music        Folk Music        Patriotic Music
```

Classical Music
- Uses musical ᵃ_____
- Symphony = long piece of music for an orchestra
- Concerto = uses an orchestra and soloists
- ᵇ_____ and choral music = involve singing

Folk Music
- Songs and music passed down for many years.
- Is fun to listen to
- Is ᶜ_____ music

Patriotic Music
- National anthems
- Makes people feel ᵈ_____ of their country

Vocabulary Builder

Write the correct words and the meanings in Chinese.

 1 ▸ a musician who performs a solo

_____

 2 ▸ music is sung by a choir

_____

 3 ▸ a large group of musicians using many different instruments to play mostly classical music

_____

 4 ▸ a kind of performance in which actors sing most of the words with music performed by an orchestra

_____

Modern Music

What kind of music do you like?

People have different tastes in music.

Some like classical music. Others like modern pop music.

Some love to sing and play music. Others like listening to music.

Let's find out more about modern music.

Jazz is a special kind of music.

When jazz musicians play, they improvise.

They change the words and the tunes while playing, so the music sounds a little different every time.

Different jazz musicians can play the same songs in different ways.

Some people call rock music "rock and roll."

Rock music often features guitars and drums.

Most rock bands have one or two singers.

Pop music is similar to rock music.

But it often features more lighthearted music.

It is also like dance music.

Rap is a fairly new type of music.

Often, rappers speak, not sing, the lyrics to their songs.

Key Words

- taste
- modern pop music
- jazz
- musician
- improvise
- tune
- rock music
- rock and roll
- band
- feature
- lighthearted
- rap
- rapper
- lyrics

 Modern Music

jazz

rock music

pop music

rap

Main Idea and Details

1   What is the passage mainly about?

   a. Classical and jazz music.

   b. The lyrics that rappers sing.

   c. Different kinds of modern music.

2   What do jazz musicians do when they play?

   a. They sing.   **b.** They improvise.   **c.** They dance.

3   What does lighthearted **mean?**

   a. Cheerful.   **b.** Fast-paced.   **c.** Unique.

4   Complete the sentences.

   a. _____ musicians change the words and music when they play.

   b. Rock musicians often play the _____ and drums.

   c. Rappers usually _____ the lyrics to their songs.

5   Complete the outline.

```
                         Modern Music
   ┌──────────┬──────────────┴──────────┬───────────┐
  Jazz      Rock and Roll          Pop Music        Rap
```

Jazz	Rock and Roll	Pop Music	Rap
• The musicians improvise. • Change the ^a_____ and tunes while playing • Music sounds ^b_____ every time they play.	• Features guitars and drums • Rock bands have one or two ^c_____.	• Is similar to rock music • Is ^d_____ • Is like dance music	• A new ^e_____ of music • Rappers usually speak the lyrics.

Vocabulary Builder

Write the correct words and the meanings in Chinese.

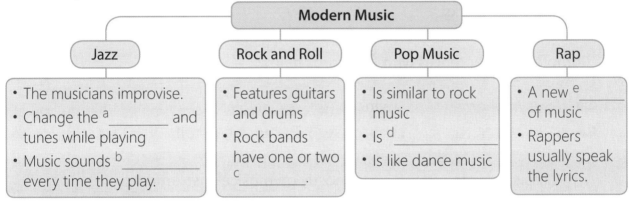

1 ▸ to perform without preparing in advance

_____

2 ▸ having or showing a cheerful and happy nature

_____

3 ▸ a group of musicians who play popular music together

_____

4 ▸ the words to a song

_____

life   is   so   great

Vocabulary ▸ Review 9

A Complete the sentences with the words below.

> geometrical   paintings   reality   realistic
> Spaniard   abstract   cubism   printmaker

1 Realistic art shows objects as they look in _____.

2 Rembrandt, a Dutch artist, was a famous _____ artist.

3 _____ paintings create images in new and unusual ways.

4 Picasso was a _____ who painted during the twentieth century.

5 Picasso painted objects in different _____ shapes.

6 One of Picasso's most famous styles was _____.

7 Picasso was also a sculptor and _____.

8 Today, people spend millions of dollars buying Picasso's _____ and other works.

B Complete the sentences with the words below.

> symphony   relies   similar   involve
> patriotic   improvise   rock and roll   lyrics

1 Classical music _____ mostly on musical instruments.

2 A long piece of music played by an orchestra is called a _____.

3 Operas and choral music are two other forms of music that _____ singing.

4 _____ music is songs and music like national anthems.

5 When jazz musicians play, they _____.

6 Some people call rock music "_____ _____ _____."

7 Pop music is _____ to rock music.

8 Often, rappers speak, not sing, the _____ to their songs.

Write the correct word and the meaning in Chinese.

1 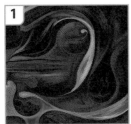 ▸ art that shows objects in a new and unusual way

_____

2  ▸ an artistic movement that featured surfaces of geometrical planes

_____

3  ▸ an artist who makes sculptures

_____

4  ▸ a musician who performs a solo

_____

5  ▸ a person who performs raps

_____

6  ▸ to perform without preparing in advance

_____

D

Match each word with the correct definition and write the meaning in Chinese.

1 separate _____ ☐

2 divide _____ ☐

3 unusual _____ ☐

4 printmaker _____ ☐

5 antiwar _____ ☐

6 choral music _____ ☐

7 patriotic _____ ☐

8 national anthem _____ ☐

9 improvise _____ ☐

10 tune _____ ☐

a. a print artist

b. music sung by a choir

c. opposed to war

d. a musical sound; a melody

e. a nation's official song

f. different; to divide or to split

g. different from what is usual or ordinary

h. to separate something into two or more parts

i. to perform without preparing in advance

j. feeling, expressing, or inspired by love for one's country

A Write the correct word for each sentence.

> lighthearted   landscape   musicians   equal groups   capital
> proverbs   ones   replace   place value   terrible

1   Number sentences _____ words with numbers.

2   We know the value of each digit because of _____ _____.

3   245 means that it has 2 hundreds, 4 tens, and 5 _____.

4   Division separates a number into _____ _____.

5   Proper nouns begin with _____ letters.

6   Some myths are stories about brave heroes and _____ monsters.

7   Common sayings or _____ often have special meanings.

8   In realistic art, the _____ would look exactly like it does in reality.

9   Pop music often features more _____ music.

10 Different jazz _____ can play the same songs in different ways.

B Write the meanings of the words in Chinese.

1	addend	_____	16	punish	_____
2	operation sign	_____	17	set free	_____
3	digit	_____	18	pass down	_____
4	quotient	_____	19	oral tradition	_____
5	factor	_____	20	patient	_____
6	figure out	_____	21	abstract art	_____
7	three-digit number	_____	22	geometrical shape	_____
8	multiple times	_____	23	sculptor	_____
9	skip count	_____	24	rapper	_____
10	omit	_____	25	separate	_____
11	goddess	_____	26	unusual	_____
12	monster	_____	27	antiwar	_____
13	proverb	_____	28	choral music	_____
14	mysterious	_____	29	patriotic	_____
15	feel sorry for	_____	30	national anthem	_____

- Word List
- Answers and Translations

Word List

01 How Transportation Has Changed

1	**technology** (n.)	技術；科技
2	**way** (n.)	方式
3	**better** (a.)	較好的 * good–better–best
4	**transportation** (n.)	交通工具
5	**thanks to**	由於
6	**wagon** (n.)	四輪運貨馬車
7	**drive** (v.)	駕駛（汽車等）
8	**ride on**	搭乘
9	**subway** (n.)	地鐵
10	**carry** (v.)	載運
11	**goods** (n.)	貨物；商品
12	**at one time**	同時地
13	**quickly** (adv.)	快速地
14	**safely** (adv.)	安全地

02 Inventors and Inventions

1	**inventor** (n.)	發明家
2	**invention** (n.)	發明；發明物
3	**communicate** (v.)	溝通
4	**especially** (adv.)	尤其
5	**laboratory** (n.)	實驗室
6	**invent** (v.)	發明
7	**hundreds of**	數百的
8	**phonograph** (n.)	留聲機
9	**motion picture camera**	電影攝影機
10	**light bulb**	燈泡
11	**light** (v.)	照亮
12	**be fascinated by**	被……吸引
13	**electric wire**	電線
14	**millions of**	數百萬；無數的

03 Choosing Our Leaders

1	**democracy** (n.)	民主國家
2	**vote** (v.)	投票
3	**government** (n.)	政府
4	**election** (n.)	選舉
5	**local** (a.)	地方的
6	**state** (a.)	州的
7	**national** (a.)	國家的
8	**run for**	競選
9	**office** (n.)	官職
10	**congressman** (n.)	國會議員
11	**adult** (a.)	成人的；成年人的
12	**at least**	至少
13	**election day**	投票日
14	**count** (v.)	計算

04 Presidents' Day in February

1	**greatest** (a.)	最偉大的 * great–greater–greatest
2	**be born**	出生
3	**celebrate** (v.)	慶祝
4	**birthday** (n.)	生日
5	**national holiday**	國定假日
6	**win** (v.)	贏；獲勝 * win–won–won
7	**Civil War**	美國內戰；南北戰爭
8	**free** (v.)	解放
9	**slave** (n.)	奴隸
10	**honor** (v.)	給……以榮譽
11	**be closed**	關閉
12	**show respect**	表示尊敬

05 Countries Have Neighbors

1	**continent** (n.)	大陸；大洲
2	**several** (a.)	數個的
3	**touch** (v.)	接觸

4	Caribbean Sea	加勒比海
5	be situated	位於
6	Cuba (n.)	古巴
7	Haiti (n.)	海地
8	Dominican Republic	多明尼加共和國
9	Russia (n.)	俄羅斯
10	Brazil (n.)	巴西
11	South America	南美洲
12	Argentina (n.)	阿根廷
13	Chile (n.)	智利
14	Columbia (n.)	哥倫比亞

6	dam (n.)	水壩
7	hold (v.)	保有；容納
8	pave (v.)	鋪、築（路等）
9	construct (v.)	建造
10	bridge (n.)	橋
11	dig in the ground	挖掘地底
12	fuel (n.)	燃料
13	be careful	小心仔細的
14	cause (v.)	引起
15	pollution (n.)	污染；污染物
16	harm (v.)	危害；傷害

06 The Amazon Rain Forest

1	be located in	座落於
2	flow (v.)	流動
3	go through	經過
4	surround (v.)	圍繞
5	enormous (a.)	廣大的
6	rain forest	（熱帶）雨林
7	amazing (a.)	令人驚訝的；驚人的
8	species (n.)	物種
9	mammal (n.)	哺乳動物
10	reptile (n.)	爬蟲類
11	tropical (a.)	熱帶的
12	tropical bird	熱帶鳥類
13	a wide variety of	種類繁多的
14	cut down	砍伐
15	destroy (v.)	破壞
16	protect (v.)	保護

07 Protecting the Earth

1	natural resource	天然資源
2	without (prep.)	沒有
3	be able to	能
4	survive (v.)	活下來
5	in many ways	以許多方式

08 The World's Endangered Animals

1	endangered (a.)	瀕臨絕種的
2	California condor	加州兀鷲
3	giant panda	大熊貓
4	Bengal tiger	孟加拉虎
5	blue whale	藍鯨
6	loggerhead turtle	赤蠵龜
7	national park	國家公園
8	watch (v.)	看護；注意
9	carefully (adv.)	小心地
10	hunting (n.)	打獵
11	strictly (adv.)	嚴格地
12	prohibit (v.)	禁止

09 World Religions

1	religion (n.)	宗教
2	follower (n.)	信仰者；信徒
3	believe in	信仰
4	Christianity (n.)	基督教
5	Jesus Christ	耶穌
6	Christian (n.)	基督教徒
7	holy book	神聖的書；聖典
8	Bible (n.)	聖經
9	Buddhism (n.)	佛教

10	**Buddhist** (n.)	佛教徒
11	**Islam** (n.)	伊斯蘭教
12	**Muhammad** (n.)	穆罕默德
13	**prophet** (n.)	先知
14	**Allah** (n.)	阿拉
15	**Islamic** (a.)	伊斯蘭教的
16	**believer** (n.)	信仰者
17	**Muslim** (n.)	伊斯蘭教徒；穆斯林
18	**Hinduism** (n.)	印度教
19	**Hindu** (n.)	印度教徒
20	**Brahma** (n.)	梵天

Religious Holidays

1	**holy** (a.)	神聖的
2	**several** (a.)	幾個的
3	**Christmas** (n.)	耶誕節
4	**Easter** (n.)	復活節
5	**December** (n.)	十二月
6	**worship** (v.)	（做）禮拜；敬神
7	**major** (a.)	主要的
8	**Resurrection** (n.)	耶穌復活
9	**come back to life**	重生
10	**Ramadan** (n.)	伊斯蘭教齋戒月（九月）
11	**last** (v.)	持續
12	**fast** (v.)	禁食

Early Travelers to America

1	**Native American**	美國原住民
2	**explorer** (n.)	探險家
3	**sail** (v.)	航行
4	**riches** (n.)	財富
5	**captain** (n.)	船長
6	**journey** (n.)	航程
7	**look for**	尋找
8	**instead** (adv.)	作為替代
9	**discover** (v.)	發現

10	**New World**	新大陸
11	**European** (n.)	歐洲人
12	**Portugal** (n.)	葡萄牙
13	**France** (n.)	法國
14	**Britain** (n.)	英國
15	**Netherlands** (n.)	荷蘭
16	**England** (n.)	英格蘭
17	**Spaniard** (n.)	西班牙人
18	**include** (v.)	包括

The Pilgrims and Thanksgiving

1	**Pilgrim** (n.)	清教徒
2	**religious** (a.)	宗教的；篤信宗教的
3	**disagree with**	不同意……
4	**in one's own way**	以自己的方式
5	**Church of England**	英國國教
6	*Mayflower* (n.)	五月花號
7	**land** (v.)	登陸
8	**settlement** (n.)	殖民地
9	**how to**	如何……
10	**Wampanoag Indians**	美國萬帕諾亞印第安人
11	**grow** (v.)	種植
12	**save** (v.)	挽救
13	**successful** (a.)	成功的
14	**invite** (v.)	邀請
15	**thank** (v.)	感謝
16	**Thanksgiving** (n.)	感恩節

Inside the Earth

1	**Earth's surface**	地球表面
2	**beneath** (prep.)	在……之下
3	**layer** (n.)	地層
4	**crust** (n.)	地殼
5	**mantle** (n.)	地函
6	**core** (n.)	地核
7	**outermost** (a.)	最外部的

8	make up	組成
9	thickest (a.)	最厚的
		*thick–thicker–thickest
10	melted (a.)	熔化的
11	meted rock	熔岩
12	deeper (a.)	較深的
		*deep–deeper–deepest
13	outer core	地核外核
14	extremely (adv.)	極端地；非常
15	liquid (n.)	液體
16	inner core	地核內核
17	solid (a.)	固體的
18	nickel (n.)	鎳

Earthquakes and Volcanoes

1	shake (v.)	搖晃；震動
2	earthquake (n.)	地震
3	powerful (a.)	強大的
4	violent (a.)	強烈的
5	crack (v.)	爆裂
6	fall (v.)	下沉
7	burst (v.)	爆炸
8	volcano (n.)	火山
9	magma (n.)	岩漿
10	erupt (v.)	爆發
11	ash (n.)	灰塵；灰燼
12	lava (n.)	熔岩
13	reach (v.)	到達
14	cool (v.)	冷卻
15	Hawaiian Islands	夏威夷群島
16	be formed	形成

Why Does the Moon Seem to Change?

1	object (n.)	物體
2	appearance (n.)	外觀
3	seem to	似乎
4	ball (n.)	球（體）

5	move around	圍繞……運行
6	like (prep.)	如同（口語用法）
7	reflect (v.)	反射
8	orbit (v.)	繞……軌道運行
9	lit (a.)	明亮的；被照亮的
		*light 的動詞三態：light-lighted/lit–lighted/lit
10	phase (n.)	【天】相
11	new moon	新月
12	first quarter	上弦月
13	full moon	滿月
14	last quarter	下弦月

The First Man on the Moon

1	Soviet Union	蘇聯
2	satellite (n.)	衛星
3	outer space	外太空
4	Space Race	太空競賽
5	declaration (n.)	宣告
6	declare (v.)	宣布
7	space program	太空計畫
8	Apollo 11	阿波羅 11 號
9	launch (v.)	發射
10	Kennedy Space Center	甘迺迪太空總署
11	lunar (a.)	月亮的
12	lunar mission	登月計畫
13	astronaut (n.)	太空人
14	orbit (n.)	運行軌道

Electricity

1	electricity (n.)	電
2	energy (n.)	能量
3	provide (v.)	提供
4	power (n.)	電力
5	glow (v.)	發亮
6	run (v.)	啟動；傳送
7	electric current	電流

8	through (prep.)	通過
9	wire (n.)	電線
10	outlet (n.)	電源插座
11	plug (n.)	插頭
12	turn on	打開
13	battery (n.)	電池
14	flashlight (n.)	手電筒

10	snail (n.)	蝸牛
11	force (n.)	力
12	gravity (n.)	地心引力
13	toward (prep.)	朝向
14	friction (n.)	摩擦力
15	rub (v.)	摩擦
16	brake (n.)	煞車

18 Conserving Electricity

1	refrigerator (n.)	冰箱
2	appliance (n.)	電器；設備
3	commonly (adv.)	通常地
4	save (v.)	節省
5	fossil fuel	化石燃料
6	supply (n.)	供應
7	limit (v.)	限制；限定
8	forever (adv.)	永遠
9	conserve (v.)	節省
10	decrease (v.)	減少
11	pollution (n.)	污染
12	air pollution	空氣污染
13	turn off	關掉
14	air conditioner	冷氣
15	heater (n.)	暖氣
16	ride a bike	騎腳踏車

20 Magnets

1	magnet (n.)	磁鐵
2	paper clip	迴紋針
3	rubber band	橡皮筋
4	bring (v.)	帶來；拿來
5	attract (v.)	吸引
6	iron (n.)	鐵
7	steel (n.)	鋼
8	plastic (n.)	塑膠
9	pole (n.)	磁極
10	north-seeking pole	北極
11	south-seeking pole	南極
12	opposite (a.)	相對的
13	repel (v.)	排斥
14	magnetized (a.)	有磁性的
15	compass needle	羅盤的指針
16	credit card	信用卡

19 Motion and Forces

1	forward (adv.)	向前
2	backward (adv.)	向後
3	curve (v.)	彎曲；以曲線行進
4	zigzag (v.)	成 Z 字形；以 Z 字形進行
5	motion (n.)	運動；移動
6	in motion	運動中；移動中
7	speed (n.)	速度
8	certain (a.)	某種（或一定）程度的
9	distance (n.)	距離

21 What Is Sound?

1	form (n.)	類型；種類
2	be made by	由……產生
3	vibration (n.)	振動
4	make sound	製造聲音
5	vibrate (v.)	振動
6	phone (n.)	電話
7	speaker (n.)	揚聲器
8	sound wave	聲波
9	loud (a.)	大聲的

10 **per** (prep.)   每

11 **per second**   每秒鐘

12 **speed of sound**   聲速；音速

22 Sounds and Safety

1 **siren** (n.)   警報器

2 **whisper** (n.)   低語；耳語；悄悄話

3 **loudness** (n.)   音量；響度

4 **whistle** (n.)   口哨；哨音

5 **pitch** (n.)   音高

6 **dislike** (v.)   不喜歡

7 **extremely** (adv.)   極端地；非常

8 **hurt** (v.)   傷害

9 **warn** (v.)   警告

10 **danger** (n.)   危險

11 **save** (v.)   挽救

12 **life** (n.)   生命

13 **fire alarm**   火災警示器

14 **smoke detector**   煙霧探測器

15 **ambulance** (n.)   救護車

16 **emergency** (n.)   緊急情況

23 The Organs of the Human Body

1 **organ** (n.)   器官

2 **unique** (a.)   獨一無二的

3 **function** (n.)   功能

4 **heart** (n.)   心臟

5 **brain** (n.)   腦

6 **lung** (n.)   肺

7 **circulatory** (a.)   循環的

8 **circulatory system**   血液循環系統

9 **pump** (v.)   一抽一吸；以幫浦方式輸送

10 **nervous** (a.)   神經的

11 **nervous system**   神經系統

12 **message** (n.)   訊息

13 **control** (v.)   控制

14 **mental** (a.)   精神上的

15 **physical** (a.)   身體上的

16 **respiratory** (a.)   呼吸的

17 **respiratory system**   呼吸系統

18 **stomach** (n.)   胃

19 **liver** (n.)   肝

20 **intestine** (n.)   腸

21 **digest** (v.)   消化

22 **chemical** (n.)   化學物質

24 The Five Senses

1 **sense** (n.)   感官

2 **the five senses**   五大感官

3 **react** (v.)   反應

4 **sight** (n.)   視覺

5 **smell** (n.)   嗅覺

6 **hearing** (n.)   聽覺

7 **taste** (n.)   味覺

8 **touch** (n.)   觸覺

9 **tongue** (n.)   舌頭

10 **sense organ**   感覺器官

11 **optic nerve**   視神經

12 **pleasant** (a.)   令人舒服（愉快）的

13 **eardrum** (n.)   鼓膜；耳膜

14 **sweet** (a.)   甜的

15 **sour** (a.)   酸的

16 **bitter** (a.)   苦的

17 **salty** (a.)   鹹的

18 **physically** (adv.)   身體上地

25 Word Problems

1 **word problem**   應用題

2 **solve** (v.)   解答

3 **figure out**   瞭解；明白；計算出

4 **beetle** (n.)   甲蟲

5 **addition problem**   加法題

6	**number sentence**	算式
7	**replace** (v.)	取代
8	**addend** (n.)	加數
9	**sum** (n.)	和
10	**picnic** (n.)	野餐
11	**subtraction problem**	減法題
12	**left over**	剩餘（下）的
13	**difference** (n.)	差
14	**operation sign**	運算符號

Place Value

1	**digit** (n.)	數字
2	**value** (n.)	數值
3	**one-digit** (a.)	一位數的；個位數的
4	**put together**	放在一起
5	**two-digit** (a.)	兩位數的
6	**three-digit** (a.)	三位數的
7	**place value**	位值
8	**determine** (v.)	決定
9	**location** (n.)	位置
10	**hundreds place**	百位數
11	**tens place**	十位數
12	**ones place**	個位數

Multiplication and Division

1	**imagine** (v.)	想像
2	**multiplication** (n.)	乘法
3	**multiply** (v.)	做乘法；相乘
4	**equal group**	等量
5	**multiple times**	多次
6	**quick** (a.)	快速的
7	**factor** (n.)	因數
8	**product** (n.)	（乘）積
9	**division** (n.)	除法
10	**separate** (v.)	分開
11	**dividend** (n.)	被除數

12	**divide** (v.)	除以
13	**divisor** (n.)	除數
14	**quotient** (n.)	商

Skip Counting Equal Groups

1	**one by one**	一個一個地
2	**skip count**	跳數
3	**by twos**	以 2 的倍數
4	**two times**	兩倍
5	**by fives**	以 5 的倍數
6	**by tens**	以 10 的倍數
7	**omit** (v.)	省略
8	**backward** (adv.)	反向地；向後
9	**easiest** (a.)	最簡單的 * easy–easier–easiest
10	**multiplication table**	九九乘法表

What Are Myths?

1	**myth** (n.)	神話
2	**mysterious** (a.)	神秘的
3	**experience** (n.)	經驗
4	**make up**	杜撰
5	**similar** (a.)	相似的
6	**goddess** (n.)	女神
7	**brave** (a.)	勇敢的
8	**hero** (n.)	英雄
9	**terrible** (a.)	可怕的
10	**monster** (n.)	怪物
11	**although** (conj.)	雖然
12	**ancient** (a.)	古代的
13	**Greek mythology**	希臘神話
14	**Roman mythology**	羅馬神話

30　Prometheus Brings Fire

1	**giant** (a.)	巨大的
2	**Titan** (n.)	【希神】泰坦
3	**order** (v.)	命令
4	**creature** (n.)	生物；動物
5	**man** (n.)	人類
6	**remain** (v.)	留下
7	**feel sorry for**	對……感到抱歉、覺得可憐
8	**furious** (a.)	狂怒的
9	**punish** (v.)	懲罰
10	**chain** (v.)	用鎖鏈綁住
11	**fly down**	飛下 * fly–flew–flown
12	**set free**	釋放

31　Nouns

1	**noun** (n.)	名詞
2	**part of speech**	詞性
3	**verb** (n.)	動詞
4	**adjective** (n.)	形容詞
5	**name** (v.)	指稱；陳說
6	**common noun**	普通名詞
7	**proper noun**	專有名詞
8	**particular** (a.)	特定的
9	**Mount Everest**	聖母峰
10	**elementary school**	小學
11	**capital letter**	大寫字母
12	**small letter**	小寫字母
13	**singular** (a.)	單數的
14	**plural** (a.)	複數的
15	**singular noun**	單數名詞
16	**plural noun**	複數名詞

32　Some Common Sayings

1	**common** (a.)	普通的；常見的
2	**common saying**	俗諺
3	**proverb** (n.)	諺語
4	**moral** (a.)	道德的
5	**wisdom** (n.)	智慧
6	**pass down**	流傳下來
7	**oral tradition**	口述傳統
8	**well-known** (a.)	眾所皆知的；知名的
9	**in a day**	一天中
10	**familiar** (a.)	熟悉的
11	**advise** (v.)	勸告
12	**patient** (a.)	耐心的
13	**practice** (n.) (v.)	練習
14	**perfect** (a.)	精通的
15	**keep** (v.)	保持；繼續不斷
16	**be good at**	擅長

33　Realistic Art and Abstract Art

1	**artist** (n.)	藝術家；畫家
2	**paint** (v.)	繪畫
3	**picture** (n.)	圖畫
4	**divide** (v.)	（劃）分
5	**separate** (a.)	分開的
6	**realistic** (a.)	寫實的
7	**realistic art**	寫實藝術
8	**abstract** (a.)	抽象的
9	**abstract art**	抽象藝術
10	**reality** (n.)	真實
11	**exactly** (adv.)	精確地
12	**real** (a.)	真實的；現實的

34　Picasso and His Work

1	**twentieth century**	二十世紀
2	**mostly** (adv.)	主要地；大部分地
3	**painting** (n.)	繪畫
4	**cubism** (n.)	立體主義
5	**geometrical shape**	幾何圖形
6	**painter** (n.)	畫家

7	sculptor (n.)	雕刻家		13	lighthearted (a.)	輕快的
8	printmaker (n.)	版畫家		14	fairly (adv.)	完全地；簡直
9	draw (v.)	畫		15	rapper (n.)	饒舌歌手
10	sketch (n.)	素描		16	lyrics (n.)	歌詞
11	antiwar (a.)	反戰的				
12	artwork (n.)	藝術作品				

35 Many Kinds of Music

1	classical music	古典音樂
2	rely on	依賴；依靠
3	popular (a.)	受歡迎的
4	piece of music	一段曲子
5	symphony (n.)	交響樂
6	concerto (n.)	協奏曲
7	soloist (n.)	獨奏者
8	opera (n.)	歌劇
9	choral music	聖歌音樂
10	involve (v.)	需要；包含
11	folk song	民謠
12	patriotic (a.)	愛國的
13	national anthem	國歌
14	feel proud of	對……感到驕傲

36 Modern Music

1	taste (n.)	愛好
2	modern (a.)	現代的
3	pop music	流行音樂
4	find out	認識
5	jazz (n.)	爵士
6	musician (n.)	音樂家
7	improvise (v.)	即興創作；即興表演
8	word (n.)	歌詞
9	tune (n.)	曲調
10	rock music	搖滾樂
11	feature (v.)	以……為特色
12	be similar to	和……相似

Answers and Translations

01 How Transportation Has Changed 交通工具如何演變？

新的技術改變了人們的生活方式。
技術就是利用科學來讓事物變得更快或更好。

讓我們來認識工業技術如何改變交通工具。
過去，乘坐馬車旅行要花好幾天的時間。
現在，人們能用許多方式更快速、更便利地旅行。
我們會駕駛汽車、卡車或巴士。
我們會搭火車或地鐵。
我們會乘船，甚至搭飛機。

許多交通工具也用來載運貨物。
卡車可以將貨物運送到國內各地。
火車可以一次載運大量貨物。
飛機和船可以將貨物運送到世界各地。

交通工具將人和貨物從一地送到其他地方。
由於這些新的技術，交通工具得以日新月異，也很安全。

- Main Idea and Details
1 **(c)**　　2 **(b)**　　3 **(c)**
4 a. **Technology**　　b. **trains**　　c. **transportation**
5 a. **wagon**　　b. **subways**　　c. **faster**　　d. **goods**
- Vocabulary Builder
1 **goods** 商品；貨物　　2 **transportation** 運輸；交通工具
3 **wagon** 四輪運貨馬車　　4 **airplane** 飛機

02 Inventors and Inventions 發明家和發明

有些人喜愛發明新東西，
我們稱他們為發明家。
他們所創造的新東西，就稱為發明物。

有些發明家大大地改變了我們的世界；
有些發明物改變了人們溝通的方式。
尤其是兩位發明家，
湯瑪士‧愛迪生和亞歷山大‧葛拉罕‧貝爾。

湯瑪士‧愛迪生是一位知名的發明家，
他每天在自己的實驗室裡努力研究。
他發明了數百種用電的物品，
包括了留聲機和電影攝影機。
我們現在使用的燈泡也是愛迪生發明的。
多虧了愛迪生，人們才得以照亮自己的家。

亞歷山大‧葛拉罕‧貝爾對聲音及其傳遞很著迷，
所以他發明了電話，
這讓我們可以透過電線交談。

今日，全世界數百萬人利用電話和遠方的親友說話，
這都是因為亞歷山大‧葛拉罕‧貝爾的緣故。

- Main Idea and Details
1 **(c)**　　2 **(b)**　　3 **(a)**　　4 **(b)**
5 a. **electric**　　b. **phonograph**　　c. **sound**　　d. **telephone**
- Vocabulary Builder
1 **invention** 發明；發明物
2 **motion picture camera** 電影攝影機
3 **laboratory** 實驗室　　4 **light bulb** 燈泡

03 Choosing Our Leaders 選出我們的首長

我們生活在民主國家，
所以我們投票選出大部分的政府首長，
我們在選舉當中進行投票。

選舉有很多種類。
在美國有地方選舉、州選舉和全國大選。
在這些選舉當中，有人出來競選各種職務。
地方選舉時，人們投票選出市長；
州選舉時，人們投票選出州長或國會議員；
全國大選時，人們選出總統。

那麼，誰可以投票？
成年公民都有投票權，
他們必須在選舉日前滿 18 歲。
每位公民可以投一票。
投票結束後會開始計票，
得票數最高的人就當選。

- Main Idea and Details
1 **(b)**　　2 **(a)**　　3 **(b)**
4 a. **People vote in elections.**
　 b. **People vote for a governor or congressmen.**
　 c. **We vote one time / once.**
5 a. **congressmen**　　b. **president**　　c. **18**　　d. **vote**
- Vocabulary Builder
1 **vote** 投票　　　　　　　2 **run for** 競選某職務
3 **adult** 成年的　　　　　　4 **count** 計算

04 Presidents' Day in February 二月的總統日

喬治‧華盛頓是美國第一任總統，
美國人尊稱他為「國父」，
許多人都視他為美國最偉大的總統。
華盛頓生於 1732 年 2 月 22 日，
就連他任內時，美國人民都年年慶祝他的生日。
不久後，這天就成為一個國定假日，
被稱為華盛頓誕辰。

亞伯拉罕‧林肯是美國的第十六任總統。
他領導贏得南北戰爭，並且解放黑奴。
林肯生於 1809 年 2 月 12 日。
林肯過世後，人民也想紀念他。

有些人就將華盛頓誕辰改名為「總統日」，
藉此紀念華盛頓和林肯兩位總統。

今日，美國人將每年二月的第三個星期一定為總統日。
學校、銀行和許多公司行號會放假一天，以紀念這兩位偉大的
美國元首。

- **Main Idea and Details**
1 **(a)**　　　2 **(c)**　　　3 **(c)**
4 a. **The father of our country.**
　b. **It's February 12, 1809.**
　c. **They're schools, banks, and many offices.**
5 a. **first**　b. **father**　c. **Civil War**　d. **slaves**　e. **February**

- **Vocabulary Builder**
1 **George Washington** 喬治‧華盛頓　　2 **free** 解放
3 **Civil War** 美國南北戰爭；美國內戰　　4 **slave** 奴隸

Vocabulary Review 1

A　1 **way**　　　　　2 **travel**
　　3 **carry**　　　　4 **goods**
　　5 **creating**　　6 **communicate**
　　7 **light**　　　　8 **telephones**

B　1 **government**　2 **elections**
　　3 **run**　　　　　4 **right**
　　5 **first**　　　　6 **born**
　　7 **Civil War**　　8 **Presidents' Day**

C　1 **transportation** 交通工具　2 **wagon** 四輪運貨馬車
　　3 **laboratory** 實驗室　　　4 **light bulb** 燈泡
　　5 **election** 選舉　　　　　6 **national holiday** 國定假日

D　1 技術；科技 **e**　　　2 地鐵 **b**
　　3 發明家 **g**　　　　4 發明 **a**
　　5 投票 **f**　　　　　6 國會議員 **d**
　　7 選舉日；大選日 **j**　8 計算 **c**
　　9 亞伯拉罕‧林肯 **h**　10 解放 **i**

05　Countries Have Neighbors 國家的鄰國

美國是北美洲的一部分，
洲是指非常大塊的陸地。
事實上，美國並不是北美洲唯一的國家，
它有許多鄰國。
美國的北邊是加拿大，
美國的南邊是墨西哥，
加拿大和墨西哥都與美國相毗鄰。

美國還有其他鄰國。
加勒比海位於它的南邊，
海上有許多島嶼，
古巴、海地和多明尼加共和國都位於此處。
此外，在北邊，還有俄國與阿拉斯加為鄰。

巴西和其鄰國位於南美洲，
巴西是南美洲面積最大的國家。
阿根廷、智利和哥倫比亞也在這裡，
這些國家都是美國的鄰國。

- **Main Idea and Details**
1 **(b)**　　　2 **(b)**　　　3 **(a)**　　　4 **(c)**
5 a. **Dominican**　b. **Russia**　c. **Brazil**　d. **Chile**

- **Vocabulary Builder**
1 **continent** 大陸；大洲　　2 **Caribbean Sea** 加勒比海
3 **beside** 在……旁邊　　　4 **be situated** 位於

06　The Amazon Rain Forest 亞馬遜雨林

亞馬遜河是世界第二長河，
它位在南美洲，
主要位於巴西，但也流經其他七個國家。
亞馬遜河周遭圍繞著廣大的雨林，
也就是亞馬遜雨林。

亞馬遜雨林是世界最大的叢林，
裡面所蘊含的生物數量驚人，
全世界有一半左右的動物物種都生活在這裡。
這裡有超過 500 種哺乳動物，將近 500 種爬蟲類，
以及大量的熱帶鳥類。
科學家認為大約有三千萬種昆蟲生活在此，
還有各式各樣的樹木、植物和花卉。

然而今日，部分的亞馬遜雨林逐漸遭到砍伐，
使得雨林的面積愈來愈小，也摧毀了許多植物和動物的家園。
我們必須保護亞馬遜雨林，
如果沒有這片雨林，數百萬的植物和動物將會滅亡。

- **Main Idea and Details**
1 **(b)**　　　2 **(b)**　　　3 **(c)**
4 a. **It flows in Brazil and seven other countries in South America.**
　b. **30 million.**
　c. **Millions of plants and animals would die.**
5 a. **seven**　b. **species**　c. **insects**　d. **destroying**

- **Vocabulary Builder**
1 **species** 物種　　　　　2 **rain forest**（熱帶）雨林
3 **jungle**（熱帶）叢林　4 **cut down** 砍伐

07　Protecting the Earth 保護地球

地球上有許多天然資源。
我們每天都在使用天然資源。
空氣、水、土壤、植物和動物都是我們所使用的重要資源，
沒有這些資源，我們就無法生存。

人類已經用許多方式改變了地球。
我們砍伐樹木來建造房子和大樓；
我們興建水壩來儲水；
我們鋪路、造橋；
我們挖地尋找煤礦、石油和天然氣等燃料。

然而，我們必須小心我們所做的改變，
有些改變可能會對地球造成傷害。
如果我們砍伐太多樹木，動物就必須尋找新的家園和食物。
如果牠們無法做到，就會死亡。

當我們製造汙染時，就危害了天然資源。
如果水和空氣不乾淨，我們就無法使用，
植物和動物也可能因而死亡。
我們必須減少資源用量，保護更多的植物和動物。

• **Main Idea and Details**

1 (a)　　　2 (c)　　　3 (a)

4 a. They're air, water, soil, plants, and animals.
　 b. We make them to hold water.
　 c. We should use fewer of natural resources.

5 a. animals　　b. dams　　c. ground　　d. homes

• **Vocabulary Builder**

1 dam 水壩　　　　　　　　2 fuel 燃料
3 pave 鋪、築（路等）　　　4 dig 挖（洞）；掘（土）

08 The World's Endangered Animals
　　世界瀕危動物

全世界有數百萬的動物，
其中有些動物已經瀕臨絕種，
亦即這些動物的存活數量非常少，
如果人類不保護牠們，牠們就可能滅亡。

現今有超過四萬種瀕危的物種，
這些動物生活在許多國家中。
加州兀鷹，一種大型鳥類，是美國瀕危的動物。
中國的大貓熊也瀕臨絕種，
印度的孟加拉虎也是。
甚至連海底動物也瀕臨絕種，
太平洋的藍鯨和大西洋的赤蠵龜就是其中兩例。

人類正在尋找保護許多瀕危動物的方法。
有些瀕危動物在國家公園裡生活，
受到嚴密地看管，
法律上是嚴禁獵捕瀕危動物的。

• **Main Idea and Details**

1 (b)　　　2 (c)　　　3 (a)

4 a. 40,000　　b. Pacific Ocean　　c. hunt

5 a. China　　b. Blue whale　　c. national　　d. Hunting

• **Vocabulary Builder**

1 endangered 瀕臨絕種的　　2 loggerhead turtle 赤蠵龜
3 national park 國家公園　　4 prohibit 禁止

Vocabulary Review 2

A　1 neighbors　　　　2 touch
　　3 Caribbean Sea　　4 South America
　　5 longest　　　　　6 enormous
　　7 species　　　　　8 variety

B　1 resources　　　　2 changed
　　3 pave　　　　　　4 problems
　　5 clean　　　　　　6 endangered
　　7 protect　　　　　8 strictly

C　1 rain forest（熱帶）雨林　　2 continent 大陸；大洲
　　3 dam 水壩　　　　　　　　4 pollution 污染；污染物
　　5 mammal 哺乳動物　　　　　6 hunting 狩獵

D　1 數個的 h　　　　　　　　2 接觸 a
　　3 位於 b　　　　　　　　　4 圍繞 g
　　5 驚人的；令人驚訝的 f　　6 砍伐 i
　　7 汙染 j　　　　　　　　　8 危害；傷害 e
　　9 瀕臨絕種的 d　　　　　　10 禁止 c

09 World Religions 世界宗教

世界上有很多宗教。
大部分宗教的信徒信仰一位或多位的神。

基督教的信徒相信耶穌基督是上帝之子，
信仰基督教的人稱為基督徒。
基督徒的神聖典籍是聖經。
基督徒會在星期日和其他特殊節日上教堂。

佛教的信徒並不信奉任何神明，
信仰佛教的人稱為佛教徒。
佛教徒相信人死後有輪迴。
許多佛教徒居住在亞洲。

伊斯蘭教的信徒相信穆罕默德是阿拉的先知。
阿拉是伊斯蘭教的真主。
信仰伊斯蘭教的人稱為穆斯林。

印度教的信仰者相信一神和眾多神祇。
印度教徒所信仰的一神是梵天，
但是他們也相信還有其他數千個神祇，
祂們都是梵天的化身或化名。

• **Main Idea and Details**

1 (c)　　　2 (c)　　　3 (b)

4 a. Bible　　b. Buddhists　　c. Hinduism

5 a. Holy book　　b. Asia　　c. prophet　　d. Hindus

• **Vocabulary Builder**

1 Bible 聖經　　　　　　2 Brahma 梵天；創造神
3 Buddhist 佛教徒　　　　4 Muslim 伊斯蘭教徒；穆斯林

10 Religious Holidays 宗教節日

每個宗教都有節日，
常被稱為宗教節日。

基督教有好幾個節日，
其中最重要的兩個是聖誕節和復活節。
聖誕節是每年的 12 月 25 日，
基督徒在聖誕節這天慶祝耶穌誕辰，
許多基督徒會在聖誕節上教堂做禮拜。
復活節是另一個主要的基督教節日，
在每年的三月底或四月初舉行。
基督徒在復活節這天慶祝耶穌復活，
他們相信耶穌在這天復活。

伊斯蘭教是另一個具有重要節日的宗教，
齋戒月是最重要的節日之一。
齋戒月為期一整個月。
齋戒月期間，伊斯蘭教徒日間必須禁食，
所以他們不能在白天進食或喝水，
等到日落之後才能進食。

- **Main Idea and Details**
1 **(b)**　　2 **(c)**　　3 **(a)**　　4 **(a)**
5 a. **Christmas**　　b. **Jesus Christ**　　c. **Muslims**

- **Vocabulary Builder**
1 **worship** 敬神；做禮拜　　2 **Easter** 復活節
3 **Resurrection** 基督復活　　4 **Ramadan** 伊斯蘭教齋戒月
　　　　　　　　　　　　　　　　　　（回曆九月）

11 Early Travelers to America
美洲的早期移民

北美洲最早的居民是印第安人，
許多年後，探險家們從歐洲前來。

其中一位早期的探險家是克里斯多弗·哥倫布。
1492 年，他從西班牙啟航，出發尋找金礦和其他寶藏。
他是三艘船艦的船長，分別是平塔號、尼尼亞號和聖瑪莉亞號。
那是一次漫長的航程，但是他終於發現了陸地。
他原本是要尋找印度，卻沒有抵達那裡。
他反而因此發現新大陸：北美洲和南美洲。

繼哥倫布之後，許多歐洲人開始航向美洲。
這些人來自許多國家，
他們分別從西班牙、葡萄牙、法國、英國和荷蘭啟航。
從英格蘭出發的約翰·卡波特就是一位探險家，
他繞著加拿大航行。
許多西班牙人航向新大陸，
這些探險家包括瓦斯科·德·巴爾伯亞和龐塞·德萊昂，
以及赫爾南多·科爾特斯等。
每一年都有越來越多人來到美洲新大陸。

- **Main Idea and Details**
1 **(c)**　　2 **(b)**　　3 **(c)**　　4 **(c)**
5 a. **Spain**　　b. **New World**　　c. **England**　　d. **Spain**

- **Vocabulary Builder**
1 **explorer** 探險家　　　　2 **captain** 船長
3 **sail** 航行；啟航　　　　4 **New World** 新大陸

12 The Pilgrims and Thanksgiving
清教徒和感恩節

清教徒是來自英國的宗教團體，
他們不認同英國國教，
想要依照自己的方式來信仰。
因此，他們決定離開英國，尋求宗教自由。

1620 年，清教徒離開英國，前往美洲。
他們乘坐的船隻稱為五月花號，
他們在美洲的麻薩諸塞一帶登陸。
清教徒在普利茅斯建立殖民地。

他們的第一個冬天艱困無比，40 個人沒有撐過那個冬天。
清教徒們不知道如何在新家園生活，
但是萬帕諾亞格印第安人救了他們。
萬帕諾亞格人教他們如何捕魚、打獵和耕種糧食。
到了秋天，清教徒有了豐富的食物，
並且成功地在美洲定居下來。
清教徒邀請美洲印第安人共享大餐，
感謝上帝賜予他們的美好一切。
這就是第一個感恩節。

- **Main Idea and Details**
1 **(b)**　　2 **(a)**　　3 **(a)**
4 a. **freedom**　　b. **1620**　　c. **Thanksgiving**
5 a. **freedom**　　b. **Landed**　　c. **Indians**　　d. **Thanksgiving**

- **Vocabulary Builder**
1 **Church of England** 英國國教會　2 **religious** 宗教的
3 **Pilgrim** 英國清教徒　　　　　4 **settlement** 定居；殖民地

Vocabulary Review 3

A 1 **religions**　　　　　2 **prophet**
　　3 **Brahma**　　　　　4 **life**
　　5 **holidays**　　　　　6 **celebrated**
　　7 **Resurrection**　　　8 **fast**

B 1 **Native Americans**　2 **Europe**
　　3 **New World**　　　　4 **sailing**
　　5 **Pilgrims**　　　　　6 **landed**
　　7 **how to**　　　　　8 **invited**

C 1 **Pilgrim** 英國清教徒　2 **Christian** 基督徒
　　3 **Easter** 復活節　　　4 **Ramadan** 伊斯蘭教齋戒月
　　5 **explorer** 探險家　　6 **captain** 船長

D 1 耶穌復活 **i**　　　　2 基督徒 **b**
　　3 伊斯蘭教徒 **a**　　　4 做禮拜 **g**
　　5 航程 **d**　　　　　6 西班牙人 **h**
　　7 不同意 **f**　　　　　8 宗教的 **c**
　　9 五月花號 **e**　　　　10 殖民地 **j**

Wrap-Up Test 1

A 1 **transportation**　　2 **inventions**
　　3 **elections**　　　　4 **endangered**
　　5 **resources**　　　　6 **Surrounding**
　　7 **religions**　　　　8 **North America**
　　9 **celebrate**　　　　10 **religious**

B 1 交通工具　　　　　2 實驗室
　　3 奴隸　　　　　　　4 技術；科技
　　5 發明家　　　　　　6 投票
　　7 國會議員　　　　　8 選舉
　　9 計算　　　　　　　10 解放
　　11 （熱帶）雨林　　　12 燃料
　　13 接觸　　　　　　　14 位於
　　15 圍繞　　　　　　　16 驚人的；令人驚訝的
　　17 砍伐　　　　　　　18 汙染；污染物

19 瀕臨絕種的　　　　20 禁止
21 聖經　　　　　　　22 佛教徒
23 復活節　　　　　　24 探險家
25 耶穌復活　　　　　26 伊斯蘭教徒；穆斯林
27 敬神；做禮拜　　　28 西班牙人
29 信仰者；信徒　　　30 殖民地

13 Inside the Earth 地球內部構造

我們住在地球的表面。
然而，地球在地表下方還有幾個不同的地層，
分別是地殼、地函和地核。

地殼是地球最外部的薄層，
是我們所居住的地球表面。
地殼由地球上所有的水和陸地所組成——包含了山脈、河川、
海洋和大陸。

地函是地殼之下的岩石層，
它是地球最厚的地層，充滿熾熱的熔岩。
事實上，地函非常熱，
越深層的地函越熱。

地球的中心是地核，
分為兩部分：外核和內核。
外核非常熾熱，主要是液態金屬。
內核主要是固態的鐵和鎳。

- **Main Idea and Details**
1 (c)　　　2 (c)　　　3 (a)
4 a. **core**　　　b. **hot**　　　c. **liquid**
5 a. **outermost**　　b. **thickest**　　c. **inner core**　　d. **solid**
- **Vocabulary Builder**
1 **layer** 層；地層　　　　　　2 **crust** 地殼
3 **mantle** 地函　　　　　　　4 **liquid metal** 液態金屬

14 Earthquakes and Volcanoes
地震和火山

有時候，地面會開始震動。
這樣的震動可能持續幾秒鐘或幾分鐘，
就是所謂的地震。
地震的發生是由於地殼構造在地底移動所造成。
大部分地震只是輕度搖晃，有的卻非常劇烈。
地震會造成道路龜裂，並摧毀建築物。
地震也會改變地球表面，
致使陸地下沉或上升。

在有些地方，熱熔岩會自地表噴發，
這就是火山。
這種被稱為岩漿的熱熔岩來自地函，
當火山爆發時，灰燼、氣體和岩漿會流到地表。
岩漿流出地表之後，就稱為熔岩。
熔岩能摧毀任何它所觸及的一切，但它也具有創造力。
位於水中的火山爆發時，流出的熔岩經常冷卻形成島嶼。
夏威夷群島就是由這種火山爆發所形成。

- **Main Idea and Details**
1 (a)　　　2 (c)　　　3 (b)　　　4 (c)
5 a. **ground**　　b. **fall**　　c. **melted rock**　　d. **Lava**
- **Vocabulary Builder**
1 **crack** 使爆裂；使破裂　　　2 **earthquake** 地震
3 **erupt** 噴出；爆發　　　　　4 **lava** 熔岩

15 Why Does the Moon Seem to Change?
為何月亮有圓缺變化？

月球是夜空中最大的物體，
但是月亮的樣貌似乎每每天都在改變。
有時可以看見全部，有時只能看見一部分，
有時完全看不到。

事實上，月亮並沒有改變形狀。
月球是一個繞行地球的巨大球體，
它不像星星一樣自己會發光，
它是反射太陽光才看起來那麼亮。
當月球繞著地球運轉時，
我們看到它被太陽照亮的部分每一夜都不同。
因此月亮看起來好像會改變形狀。

月亮的各種不同形狀被稱為月相。
月亮的四個主要月相分別是：新月、上弦月、滿月和下弦月。
所有月相變化一輪的週期大約是 29 天。

- **Main Idea and Details**
1 (b)　　　2 (a)　　　3 (b)
4 a. **It's a huge ball of rock that moves around Earth.**
　　b. **It called the phases of the moon.**
　　c. **They're new moon, first quarter, full moon, and last quarter.**
5 a. **sun's light**　　b. **Earth**　　c. **last quarter**
- **Vocabulary Builder**
1 **phase** 【天】相　　　　　2 **reflect** 反射；映出
3 **orbit** 繞……軌道運行　　　4 **last quarter** 下弦月

16 The First Man on the Moon
登上月球的第一人

1957 年 10 月 4 日，蘇聯發射衛星到外太空，
開啟了蘇聯和美國之間的太空競賽。

接著，約翰‧甘迺迪總統於 1961 年發表聲明，
宣布美國將於 1960 年代結束前，將人類送上月球。
之後，美國太空計劃便開始讓多名太空人進入太空。

終於在 1969 年時，美國的登月計劃準備就緒。
7 月 16 日那天，「阿波羅 11 號」從美國甘迺迪太空總署發射
升空。
這是美國太空總署（NASA）阿波羅計劃的第三次月球任務。
四天後，於 7 月 20 日，「阿波羅 11 號」讓首位人類登上月球。
尼爾‧阿姆斯壯和巴茲‧艾德林是史上首次登陸月球的人類，
而太空人麥可‧科林斯則繼續繞行月球軌道。
7 月 24 日，三名太空人平安返回地球。

- Main Idea and Details

1 (c)　　　2 (a)　　　3 (a)

4 a. United States　　　b. Kennedy　　　c. *Apollo 11*

5 a. Soviet Union　　　b. moon　　　c. Launched　　　d. walked

- Vocabulary Builder

1 lunar 月亮的；月球上的　　　2 mission 任務

3 launch 發射　　　4 astronaut 太空人

Vocabulary Review 4

A 　1 layer　　　　　　2 melted rock
　　3 core　　　　　　4 solid
　　5 underground　　6 surface
　　7 erupts　　　　　8 lava

B 　1 object　　　　　2 ball
　　3 reflects　　　　4 phases
　　5 space　　　　　6 Space Center
　　7 lunar　　　　　8 humans

C 　1 crust 地殼　　　　　　2 outer core（地核）外核
　　3 earthquake 地震　　　4 volcano 火山
　　5 satellite 衛星　　　　6 full moon 滿月

D 　1 最外部的 b　　　　2 地函 c
　　3 持續 g　　　　　　4 強烈的 i
　　5 外觀 e　　　　　　6 反射 d
　　7 繞……軌道運行 a　8 滿月 f
　　9 外太空 j　　　　　10 發射 h

17 Electricity 電

電是一種能量形式，
它提供電力讓許多物品能夠運轉。
因為有了電，燈泡才能發光，收音機能播放音樂。
電話也要有電才能傳送聲音。
你需要電才能開電腦和看電視，
沒有電，我們每天使用的很多東西都無法運作。

電流經由電線傳輸，
電線將電力傳到你的家中和學校。
電力從電源插座出來，沿著插頭和電線，送到電器當中。
當你打開家中的燈，電力就會透過電線傳到燈泡上。

你也可以用電池來取得電力。
手電筒需要電才能發亮，
但是你不需要插電，
只要裝上電池就可以了。
電池可以儲存能量，再將能量轉換為電力。

- Main Idea and Details

1 (a)　　　2 (b)　　　3 (b)　　　4 (a)

5 a. Electricity　　　b. wire　　　c. outlets　　　d. energy

- Vocabulary Builder

1 glow 發光　　　　2 wire 電線

3 outlet 電源插座　　4 plug 插頭

18 Conserving Electricity 節約用電

冰箱、電視、電腦和電燈都需要用電，
還有許多我們常用的其他電器也需要電。

為什麼節約用電很重要呢？
我們使用化石燃料，例如煤礦、石油和天然氣來發電，
但是化石燃料的供應有限，
一旦被用盡，就再也沒有了。
所以我們必須節約使用，
才能讓地球上的化石燃料能供應更久，
而且也可以減少空氣污染。

我們該如何節約用電呢？
有許多方法可行。
當我們不使用電燈、電腦和電視時，就把電源關掉。
不要將冰箱門打開太久，
夏天少吹冷氣，
冬天暖氣溫度不要調太高。
出門儘量搭公車、火車或騎腳踏車。

- Main Idea and Details

1 (c)　　　2 (b)　　　3 (a)

4 a. They're coal, oil, and gas.
　b. By saving electricity.
　c. We should use air conditioners less often.

5 a. appliances　　　b. supply　　　c. refrigerators
　d. air conditioners

- Vocabulary Builder

1 refrigerator 冰箱　　　2 appliance 電器；設備

3 decrease 減少；減小　　4 conserve 保存；節省

19 Motion and Forces 移動和外力

物體移動的方式有很多種，
物體可以前後移動，弧形或 Z 字形移動。
當某物體移動時，我們就說它在運動。

不同的物體有不同的移動速度。
速度是物體在一定的距離所移動的快慢。
蝸牛以非常慢的速度移動，
飛機以非常快的速度移動。

很多物體受到一點小小的力就可以移動。
力是讓物體移動的推力或拉力。
力可以改變物體的運動和速度。
地心引力是力的一種，
地心引力是將物體拉向地球的力，
東西會掉到地上是因為受到地心引力的牽引。
兩個物體互相摩擦就會產生摩擦力。
摩擦力可以使運動中的物體減速，或者完全停止。
腳踏車的煞車就是運用摩擦力的原理，來讓腳踏車停下。

- Main Idea and Details

1 (c)　　　2 (a)　　　3 (c)

4 a. speeds　　　b. gravity　　　c. down

5 a. forward　　　b. distance　　　c. pull　　　d. Earth

- **Vocabulary Builder**

1 **speed** 速度	2 **motion**（物體的）運動；移動
3 **gravity** 地心引力	4 **zigzag** 成之字形；以之字形行進

20 Magnets 磁鐵

磁鐵會吸引物體靠近。
將一些迴紋針、橡皮筋或筆放在桌上，
拿一個磁鐵靠近它們，哪些東西會被它吸走呢？

磁鐵會吸引鐵製品或鋼製品，
但是磁鐵不會吸引塑膠、紙類或橡膠。
磁鐵也會排斥或吸引其他磁鐵。

所有的磁鐵都有兩個磁極，
N 代表向北的磁極，
S 代表向南的磁極。
異極會相吸，
如果一個磁鐵的北極，靠近另一個磁鐵的南極，
它們會互相吸引。
同極會相斥，
如果把兩個北極或兩個南極放在一起，
它們會互相排斥。

磁鐵被我們廣泛利用，
其中最實用的物品之一就是指南針，
它的磁針可以指出我們所前進的方位。
電腦磁碟片和電視都有磁力裝置，
信用卡和金融卡上也有磁條。

- **Main Idea and Details**

1 **(b)**　　2 **(c)**　　3 **(b)**　　4 **(b)**

5 a. **iron**　b. **attract/pull**　c. **magnetized**　d. **credit cards**

- **Vocabulary Builder**

1 **magnet** 磁鐵	2 **pole** 磁極
3 **repel** 排斥	4 **compass needle** 羅盤磁針

Vocabulary Review 5

A　1 **power**　　　　　　2 **through**
　　3 **electric machines**　4 **store**
　　5 **electricity**　　　6 **limited**
　　7 **air conditioner**　8 **heater**

B　1 **forward**　　　　2 **motion**
　　3 **pull**　　　　　4 **toward**
　　5 **rub**　　　　　6 **attract**
　　7 **repel**　　　　8 **magnetized**

C　1 **electric current** 電流　2 **flashlight** 手電筒
　　3 **appliance** 電器；設備　4 **gravity** 地心引力
　　5 **friction** 摩擦力　　6 **magnet** 磁鐵

D　1 發光 **d**　　　　2 電線 **i**
　　3 電器；設備 **j**　4 化石燃料 **c**
　　5 空氣污染 **e**　　6 速度 **b**
　　7 力；外力 **g**　　8 吸引 **h**
　　9 排斥 **a**　　　10 羅盤；指南針 **f**

21 What Is Sound? 何謂聲音？

聲音是振動所產生的一種能量形式，
若要產生聲音，就必須讓某物移動。

當你打鼓時，鼓因為振動而發出聲音。
因為電話裡的小型揚聲器振動，所以我們聽到電話響。
所有的物體振動時都會發出聲音，
當振動停止，聲音也停止。

聲音經由空氣傳導。
當某個物體振動時，周圍的空氣也隨之振動，
進而產生聲波。
當聲波傳到你耳朵時，你便聽到聲音。
聲音可以大聲或輕柔，也有高低音之分，
不過都是由聲波所造成。

聲音移動的速度非常快，
每秒可達 340 公尺，
我們稱之為音速。
現在，許多飛機的速度比音速還快。

- **Main Idea and Details**

1 **(b)**　　2 **(b)**　　3 **(c)**

4 a. **It's a form of energy made by vibrations.**
　b. **It travels through the air.**　c. **Many airplanes can.**

5 a. **vibrate**　b. **stop**　c. **air**　d. **second**

- **Vocabulary Builder**

1 **vibrate** 振動	2 **sound waves** 聲波
3 **ring**（鐘、鈴等）鳴、響	4 **speed of sound** 聲速；音速

22 Sounds and Safety 聲音和安全

聲音有許多種類。
聲音可以大聲或輕柔，可有高低音之分。
警報器的聲音很響亮；悄悄話就很輕柔。
響度是指音量的大小。
口哨的所發出的聲音很高，
音高是指聲音的高低。

很多人不喜歡很大的聲音，
有些非常巨大的聲音甚至可能傷害我們的耳朵。
但是並非所有響亮的聲音都是不好的，
有些聲音被用來警示危險。
事實上，有些巨大的聲響可以救人一命。

火災警報器可以發出極大的聲響，
告訴大家往安全的地方逃生。
煙霧探測器的功能和火災警報器很類似，
只要有濃煙產生，它們會發出巨大的聲響。
救護車和警車上也有配置聲音響亮的警笛和警示燈，
用來警示路上的其他駕駛人，有緊急事故發生。

- **Main Idea and Details**

1 **(c)**　　2 **(c)**　　3 **(b)**

4 a. **It makes a loud sound.**
　b. **They can hurt people's ears.**
　c. **The ambulances and police cars have.**

5 a. **Siren**　b. **Whistle**　c. **detectors**　d. **emergency**

- **Vocabulary Builder**

1 **siren** 警報器   2 **warn** 警告

3 **smoke detector** 煙霧探測器   4 **ambulance** 救護車

23 The Organs of the Human Body 人體器官

人體有許多不同的器官，
每個器官都有自己獨特的功能，
同時也會互相合作，構成一些器官系統。

幾個最重要的器官是心臟、腦和肺臟。
心臟是循環系統的一部分，
它將血液輸往身體各部位。
腦主管人體的神經系統，
將訊息傳至身體各部位，
同時控制了精神活動和身體活動。
肺是呼吸系統的一部分，
它讓你能夠呼吸。

胃、肝和腸幫助身體消化食物。
胃負責分解食物。
肝會製造化學物質，再將這些化學物質送到小腸，
幫助小腸進一步消化食物。
肝也有淨化血液的功能。
大腸和小腸負責吸收食物中的營養。

- **Main Idea and Details**

1 **(a)**   2 **(b)**   3 **(c)**   4 **(b)**

5 a. **Heart**   b. **breathe**   c. **Stomach**   d. **Intestines**

- **Vocabulary Builder**

1 **organ** 器官   2 **intestine** 腸

3 **brain** 腦   4 **respiratory** 呼吸的

24 The Five Senses 五大感官

五大感官協助你對周遭環境作出反應，
它們分別是視覺、嗅覺、聽覺、味覺和觸覺。
而眼睛、鼻子、耳朵、舌頭和皮膚則是身體的感覺器官。

你用眼睛來觀看。
視神經協助你看到東西，
多虧有視覺，你才能讀書、看電影、從事其他活動。

你用鼻子來嗅聞。
世界上有各種氣味，
有的宜人，有的不好太聞。

你的耳朵讓你可以聽見周圍的聲音。
聲音在空氣中以聲波的形式傳遞，
當一些聲波傳入你的耳朵時，會使鼓膜振動，你便聽見聲音。

你的舌頭幫你品嘗飲食的味道。
甜、酸、苦、鹹是四種主要的味道。

你的皮膚讓你有觸覺。
你的身體可以感覺到事物，尤其是透過你的觸覺。

- **Main Idea and Details**

1 **(c)**   2 **(c)**   3 **(b)**

4 a. **see**   b. **smells**   c. **touch**

5 a. **eyes**   b. **nose**   c. **ears**   d. **tongue**   e. **skin**

- **Vocabulary Builder**

1 **sense organs** 感覺器官   2 **lens** 水晶體

3 **bitter** 有苦味的；苦的   4 **eardrum** 鼓膜；耳膜

Vocabulary Review 6

A 1 energy   2 vibrate

    3 loud   4 speed of sound

    5 pitch   6 hurt

    7 warns   8 Ambulances

B 1 function   2 circulatory

    3 brain   4 intestines

    5 react   6 sight

    7 tongue   8 physically

C 1 sound waves 聲波   2 fire alarm 火災報警器

    3 siren 警報器   4 lung 肺

    5 tongue 舌頭   6 eardrum 鼓膜；耳膜

D 1 振動 h   2 大聲的 b

    3 聲速；音速 e   4 低語；耳語；私語 j

    5 警告 i   6 神經的 c

    7 胃 g   8 呼吸的 a

    9 感覺器官 f   10 視神經 d

Wrap-Up Test 2

A 1 crust   2 mantle

    3 phases   4 launched

    5 Electricity   6 force

    7 occurs   8 Earth

    9 vibrations   10 organs

B 1 地殼   16 速度

    2（地核）內核   17 力

    3 熔岩   18 地心引力

    4 衛星   19 吸引

    5 太空人   20 排斥

    6 最外部的   21 聲波

    7 強烈的；猛烈的   22 器官

    8 外觀   23 舌頭

    9 反射   24 鼓膜；耳膜

    10 發射   25 振動

    11 發光   26 低語；耳語；私語

    12 電線   27 神經的

    13 電器；設備   28 胃

    14 化石燃料   29 視神經

    15 空氣汙染   30 感覺器官

25 Word Problems 數學應用題

當你在練習數學時，會做到許多應用題。
在做應用題的時候，你必須要瞭解該題目要你做什麼。

這道應用題要你算什麼？
　　有五隻甲蟲在葉子上，不久又有七隻甲蟲加入，
　　現在總共有幾隻甲蟲在葉子上？

這是一個加法題。
為了要解題，你可以寫下這樣的算式：5 + 7 = 12
算式用數字取代文字敘述。
你所相加的數字 5 和 7，稱作加數。
你所得到的答案 12，稱作「和」。

現在讓我們來做另一道應用題：
　　凱文帶了十塊餅乾來野餐，他吃了四塊，請問還剩下幾塊？

這是一個減法題。
為了要解題，你可以寫下這樣的算式：10 – 4 = 6
你所得到的答案 6，稱作「差」。

這些算式中所出現的符號，例如加號、減號和等號，
稱作運算符號。

- **Main Idea and Details**

1 **(c)**　　 2 **(a)**　　 3 **(b)**

4 a. **addition**　　 b. **minus**　　 c. **figure out**

5 a. **problem**　 b. **subtract**　 c. **addends**　 d. **difference**

- **Vocabulary Builder**

1 **figure out** 理解；明白；計算出　 2 **work problem** 應用題

3 **addend** 加數　　　　　　　 4 **difference** 差

26 Place Value 數字位值

數學裡有十個數字，
分別是 0, 1, 2, 3, 4, 5, 6, 7, 8, 9，
每一個數字都有一個數值。

0 到 9 是個位數。
兩個數字組合在一起就是兩位數，
例如：10 就是兩位數的數字。
兩位數的數值介於 10 到 99 之間。

三位數一共有三個數字，
例如：100 就是三位數的數字。
三位數的數值介於 100 到 999 之間。

我們可以知道每個數字的數值，是根據它的位值。
一個數字的數值，是由它的位置所決定的。
以數字 245 為例：
2 位於百位數，所以它的數值是 200。
4 位於十位數，所以它的數值是 40。
5 位於個位數，所以它的數值是 5。
換句話說，245 就是 2 個 100，加 4 個 10，再加 5 個 1 所
組成。

- **Main Idea and Details**

1 **(a)**　　 2 **(b)**　　 3 **(a)**　　 4 **(a)**

5 a. **one-digit**　　 b. **hundreds**　 c. **tens**　 d. **ones**

- **Vocabulary Builder**

1 **digit** 數字　　　　　 2 **place value** 位值

3 **two-digit number** 兩位數　 4 **three-digit number** 三位數

27 Multiplication and Division 乘法和除法

想像你有五袋橘子，每袋各有三顆，
那麼，你總共有幾顆橘子？
你可以把它們像這樣加起來：3 + 3 + 3 + 3 + 3 = 15
也可以用乘法運算：5 x 3 = 15
當你把數字相乘時，等於是把同一數字連加好幾次。
乘法比同樣的數字累加更為快速。
當你做乘法時，相乘的數字叫做因數，
答案則稱為積。

現在，想像你有 20 顆蘋果，
你想把它們等分成四堆。
你可以利用除法得到答案，20 ÷ 4 = 5，
也就是將蘋果等分成四堆，每堆五顆蘋果。

除法是將一個數字分成幾個等份。
被除的大數字稱為被除數，
除以前者的數字稱為除數，
所得的答案為商。

- **Main Idea and Details**

1 **(b)**　　 2 **(a)**　　 3 **(c)**

4 a. **It is adding equal groups of numbers multiple
　　 times.**
　 b. **They're called the factors.**
　 c. **It is separating a number into equal groups.**

5 a. **multiple times**　 b. **product**　 c. **equal groups**
　 d. **Dividend**

- **Vocabulary Builder**

1 **factors** 因數　　　　　 2 **multiply** 乘；使相乘

3 **dividend** 被除數　　　 4 **quotient** 商

28 Skip Counting Equal Groups
　　跳數運算

有時候，我們會想要快速計算。
一個一個數可能會很慢，
但是如果我們跳著數，就快得多了。
讓我們從 1 數到 10：1, 2, 3, 4, 5, 6, 7, 8, 9, 10。
現在則用跳數的方法，以 2 的倍數數到 10：2, 4, 6, 8, 10。
以 2 為倍數跳數的話，速度是一個一個數的兩倍。

現在，我們以 5 為倍數來跳數：
5, 10, 15, 20, 25, 30, 35, 40, 45, 50
再以 10 為倍數來跳數：
10, 20, 30, 40, 50, 60, 70, 80, 90, 100

每當我們跳數時，我們會省略其他數字。
如果要數到很大的數字，這種方法會很快。
我們甚至可以倒著跳數，
以 2 為倍數倒著跳數：10, 8, 6, 4, 2, 0

學習跳數最簡單的方法是什麼？
就是學習九九乘法表。
這個表可以教你以不同數字為倍數來跳數。

• **Main Idea and Details**

1 **(c)**　　　2 **(c)**　　　3 **(a)**

4 a. **faster**　　b. **numbers**　　c. **multiplication**

5 a. **count**　　b. **quickly**　　c. **how to**

• **Vocabulary Builder**

1 **skip count** 跳數　　　　　2 **omit** 省略

3 **backward** 向後；反向地　　4 **multiplication table** 九九乘法表

Vocabulary Review 7

A　1 **word problem**　　　　2 **sentences**
　　3 **left**　　　　　　　　4 **digit**
　　5 **place value**　　　　　6 **determined**
　　7 **two-digit**　　　　　　8 **hundreds**

B　1 **multiple times**　　　2 **multiplied**
　　3 **equal groups**　　　　4 **divided**
　　5 **Skip counting**　　　　6 **fives**
　　7 **omit**　　　　　　　　8 **multiplication**

C　1 **addend** 加數　　　　2 **operation sign** 運算符號
　　3 **digit** 數字　　　　　4 **product** （乘）積
　　5 **divisor** 除數
　　6 **multiplication table** 九九乘法表

D　1 理解；明白；計算出 **b**　　2 代替 **g**
　　3 放在一起 **c**　　　　　4 兩位數字 **h**
　　5 三位數字 **i**　　　　　6 多次 **a**
　　7 跳數 **e**　　　　　　　8 除數 **d**
　　9 省略 **f**　　　　　　　10 向後；反向地 **j**

29　What Are Myths? 何謂神話？

神話是已經流傳數千年，甚至更久的故事。
很久以前，人們認為世界非常神秘。
他們不了解自己眼見和經歷的許多事，
所以經常編造故事。
這些故事說明了他們所生活的世界。
今日，我們稱這些故事為神話。

世界各地都有神話，
很多神話也很類似，
故事裡通常有男女眾神。
有些神話是關於英勇的英雄和可怕怪物的故事。
有些神話解釋了世界的起源、為什麼我們有四季，
以及人類死後會怎麼樣。
雖然我們不相信這些故事，但我們仍然樂於閱讀，
因為這些故事都非常精彩。

最著名的一些神話故事來自古希臘和古羅馬，
我們稱之為希臘羅馬神話。

• **Main Idea and Details**

1 **(a)**　　2 **(c)**　　3 **(b)**　　4 **(b)**

---

5 a. **experienced**　　b. **goddesses**　　c. **seasons**　　d. **Greek**

• **Vocabulary Builder**

1 **mysterious** 神秘的　　　　2 **brave** 勇敢的

3 **monster** 怪物　　　　　　4 **myth/mythology** 神話

30　Prometheus Brings Fire
普羅米修斯神盜火

這是一則關於人類取得火源的希臘神話。

從前，只有巨大的泰坦和眾神居住在地球上。
普羅米修斯神是一個泰坦。
有一天，眾神之王宙斯找普羅米修斯和他的兄弟艾皮米修斯談話。
宙斯命令他們創造一些新生物，
艾皮米修斯創造了許多動物，
並且賦予這些動物一些才能。
普羅米修斯只創造了一種生物：人類。
他花了很多時間創造人類，
因此沒有留給人類任何才能。

地球上的人類沒有火，感到非常寒冷。
普羅米修斯覺得人類很可憐，
便從眾神那裡偷火給地球上的人類。
宙斯發現普羅米修斯的作為之後，非常的憤怒。
為了懲罰他，宙斯用鐵鍊將他綑綁在一塊大石上。
老鷹每天都飛來咬食他的肝臟。
多年以後，普羅米修斯終於被偉大的英雄海克力斯所釋放。

• **Main Idea and Details**

1 **(b)**　　2 **(b)**　　3 **(c)**

4 a. **Zeus was.**　　b. **Because he felt sorry for them.**
　c. **Heracles did.**

5 a. **animals**　　b. **man**　　c. **fire**　　d. **chained**

• **Vocabulary Builder**

1 **Titan** 【希神】泰坦　　　2 **punish** 懲罰

3 **creature** 生物；動物　　　4 **set free** 釋放

31　Nouns 名詞

名詞和動詞、形容詞一樣，是詞性的一種。
名詞用來指人、地方或東西，
「約翰」、「城市」和「書」都是名詞。

名詞分為普通名詞和專有名詞。
普通名詞指任何人、地方或東西，
「女孩」、「學校」和「鉛筆」是普通名詞。
專有名詞指特定的人、地方或東西，
「茱麗」、「聖母峰」、「中央小學」是專有名詞。
專有名詞的第一個字母要大寫，
普通名詞則全部小寫。

名詞有單數名詞和複數名詞之分。
單數名詞是指只有一個，
複數名詞是指有兩個以上。

我們通常在單數名詞的後面加上 s、es 或 ies，來構成複數名詞。
boy、watch、story 是單數名詞。
boys、watches、stories 是複數名詞。

- **Main Idea and Details**

1 **(b)**　　2 **(a)**　　3 **(c)**

4 a. **person**　　b. **small**　　c. **plural**

5 a. **any**　　b. **particular**　　c. **Singular**　　d. **-ies**

- **Vocabulary Builder**

1 **part of speech** 詞性　　2 **proper noun** 專有名詞

3 **common noun** 普通名詞　　4 **plural noun** 複數名詞

32 Some Common Sayings 常見的諺語

每個文化都有俗諺或諺語，
俗諺或諺語通常有特殊的含意。
它們傳遞了道德啟示，
有時也帶有值得我們學習的智慧。
許多格言或諺語是經由口耳代代相傳下來的。

英文有很多俗諺。
「金窩銀窩，不如自己的狗窩。」是一句眾所皆知的諺語，
人們用這句諺語來表達旅行雖然愉快，但還是自己的家好。

「羅馬不是一天造成的。」是另一個大家所熟知的諺語。
這句諺語告誡我們做事要有耐心，欲速則不達，
所以做任何事要慢慢來、要有耐心。

「熟能生巧。」也是一句常聽到的諺語，
這句諺語告訴我們要努力不懈。
我們嘗試某個新事物的時候，通常並不擅長。
但是只要靠著練習，就能上手。

- **Main Idea and Details**

1 **(c)**　　2 **(a)**　　3 **(b)**　　4 **(c)**

5 a. **messages**　　b. **oral**　　c. **built**　　d. **Practice**

- **Vocabulary Builder**

1 **proverb** 諺語　　2 **wisdom** 智慧

3 **oral tradition** 口述傳統　　4 **pass down** 流傳下來

Vocabulary Review 8

A　1 **Myths**　　　　2 **heroes**
　　3 **how**　　　　4 **ancient**
　　5 **titans**　　　　6 **creature**
　　7 **stole**　　　　8 **punish**

B　1 **part of speech**　　2 **common noun**
　　3 **capital**　　　　4 **adding**
　　5 **sayings**　　　　6 **passed down**
　　7 **familiar**　　　　8 **perfect**

C　1 **goddess** 女神　　2 **hero** 英雄
　　3 **punish** 懲罰　　4 **proper noun** 專有名詞
　　5 **plural noun** 複數名詞　　6 **proverb** 諺語

D　1 神秘的 **e**　　　　2 古代的 **g**
　　3 對……感到抱歉、可憐 **c**　　4 懲罰 **i**
　　5 釋放 **b**　　　　6 普通名詞 **d**

7 單數名詞 **f**　　　　8 流傳下來 **a**
9 口述傳統 **j**　　　　10 耐心的 **h**

33 Realistic Art and Abstract Art 寫實藝術和抽象藝術

畫家創作各式各樣的畫作。
我們可以將藝術分成兩大派別：寫實藝術和抽象藝術。

寫實藝術呈現物體實際的樣貌。
在寫實藝術當中，風景畫就是我們現實中所看到的風景，
因此畫裡的樹木、山脈、河流看起來都非常寫實。
荷蘭畫家林布蘭就是著名的寫實藝術家。

抽象藝術所呈現的物體則和真實世界不同。
抽象畫是以全新而獨特的方式創作影像，
舉例來說，抽象風景畫並非現實中所看到的風景，
樹木可能是一團團綠球，
山脈可能是咖啡色的三角形，
河流可能是藍色的線條。
它們完全不像真實世界裡的樹木、高山和河流。

- **Main Idea and Details**

1 **(a)**　　2 **(a)**　　3 **(c)**

4 a. **It would look like it does in reality.**
　　b. **Rembrandt was.**　　c. **He was an abstract artist.**

5 a. **reality**　　b. **Rembrandt**　　c. **Trees**　　d. **Picasso**

- **Vocabulary Builder**

1 **artist** 藝術家；畫家　　2 **landscape** 風景；風景畫

3 **unusual** 獨特的　　4 **abstract art** 抽象藝術

34 Picasso and His Work 畢卡索和他的創作

偉大的藝術家有很多，
巴勃羅・畢卡索就是其中一位。
畢卡索是二十世紀的西班牙畫家。

畢卡索的畫作運用了許多不同的風格，
其中最著名的風格之一是立體主義。
他用各種不同的幾何圖形來繪製物體，
因此他的畫作裡會出現正方形、長方形和三角形。

畢卡索不僅僅是位畫家，
同時也是雕刻家和版畫家，
他甚至畫過許多素描作品，
他對不同藝術領域都感興趣。

他最知名的畫作之一叫做《格爾尼卡》，
是一幅大型的畫作，
這幅畫反映了他內心的反戰意識。

畢卡索一生創作了數以千計的藝術作品。
現今，人們願意花數百萬元購買他的畫作和其他創作。

- **Main Idea and Details**

1 **(b)**　　2 **(b)**　　3 **(c)**

4 a. **twentieth**　　b. **sculptor**　　c. **antiwar**

5 a. **Cubism**　　b. *Guernica*　　c. **printmaker**　　d. **artworks**

• **Vocabulary Builder**

1 **cubism** 立體主義
2 **sculptor** 雕刻家
3 **printmaker** 版畫家
4 **sketch** 素描

35 Many Kinds of Music 音樂類型

音樂有許多不同的類型，
其中有一種是古典音樂。
古典樂多半仰賴樂器演奏，
鋼琴、小提琴、大提琴和長笛都是常見的古典樂演奏樂器。

古典音樂也分很多種形式，
由管弦樂團演奏的長篇音樂稱作交響樂。
協奏曲也是寫給管弦樂團演奏的，
但其中會有獨奏的部分。
歌劇和聖歌音樂則是兩種需要演唱的音樂類型。

民謠是一種流傳多年的歌曲。
每個國家都有自己的民謠。
民謠通常聽起來很愉快。
大部分的傳統音樂屬於民謠。

愛國音樂是像國歌之類的歌曲或音樂。
愛國音樂可以激發人民對國家感到光榮。

• **Main Idea and Details**

1 (b)   2 (a)   3 (a)   4 (b)
5 a. **instruments**   b. **Operas**   c. **traditional**   d. **proud**

• **Vocabulary Builder**

1 **soloist** 獨奏者
2 **choral music** 聖歌音樂
3 **orchestra** 管弦樂團
4 **opera** 歌劇

36 Modern Music 現代音樂

你喜歡什麼類型的音樂？
每個人的音樂喜好都不同，
有的人喜歡古典樂，有的人喜歡現代流行音樂。
有的人愛唱歌和演奏音樂，也有人只愛聽音樂。
現在讓我們來認識現代音樂。

爵士樂是一種特別的音樂，
爵士樂手在演出時，會即興表演。
他們一邊表演，會一邊改變歌詞或旋律，
所以一首音樂每次聽起來都會有點不一樣。
不同的爵士樂手對同一首歌也會有不同的詮釋。

有人稱搖滾樂為「rock and roll」。
搖滾樂的特色通常是使用吉他和鼓，
大部分的搖滾樂團有一至兩位主唱。

流行音樂和搖滾音樂很類似，
但是流行音樂通常更為輕快，
也有點像舞曲。

饒舌樂是近年崛起的新音樂風格，
通常饒舌歌手是唸歌詞而不是唱歌。

• **Main Idea and Details**

1 (c)   2 (b)   3 (a)

4 a. **Jazz**   b. **guitar**   c. **speak**
5 a. **words** b. **different** c. **singers** d. **lighthearted** e. **type**

• **Vocabulary Builder**

1 **improvise** 即興創作；即興表演
2 **lighthearted** 輕快的
3 **band** 樂團
4 **lyrics** 歌詞

Vocabulary Review 9

A 1 **reality**   2 **realistic**
  3 **Abstract**   4 **Spaniard**
  5 **geometrical**   6 **cubism**
  7 **printmaker**   8 **paintings**

B 1 **relies**   2 **symphony**
  3 **involve**   4 **Patriotic**
  5 **improvise**   6 **rock and roll**
  7 **similar**   8 **lyrics**

C 1 **abstract art** 抽象藝術   2 **cubism** 立體主義
  3 **sculptor** 雕刻家   4 **soloist** 獨奏者
  5 **rapper** 饒舌歌手   6 **improvise** 即興創作、表演

D 1 分開的 **f**   2 （劃）分 **h**
  3 獨特的 **g**   4 版畫家 **a**
  5 反戰的 **c**   6 聖歌音樂 **b**
  7 愛國的 **j**   8 國歌 **e**
  9 即興創作；即興表演 **i**   10 曲調 **d**

Wrap-Up Test 3

A 1 **replace**   2 **place value**
  3 **ones**   4 **equal groups**
  5 **capital**   6 **terrible**
  7 **proverbs**   8 **landscape**
  9 **lighthearted**   10 **musicians**

B 1 加數   16 懲罰
  2 運算符號   17 釋放
  3 數字   18 流傳下來
  4 商   19 口述傳統
  5 因數   20 耐心的
  6 計算出   21 抽象藝術
  7 三位數   22 幾何圖形
  8 多次   23 雕刻家
  9 跳數   24 饒舌歌手
  10 省略   25 分割
  11 女神   26 獨特的
  12 怪物   27 反戰的
  13 諺語   28 聖歌音樂
  14 神秘的   29 愛國的
  15 對……感到抱歉 30 國歌

FÜN學 美國英語閱讀課本 3
各學科實用課文

Authors

Michael A. Putlack
Michael A. Putlack graduated from Tufts University in Medford, Massachusetts, USA, where he got his B.A. in History and English and his M.A. in History. He has written a number of books for children, teenagers, and adults.

e-Creative Contents
A creative group that develops English contents and products for ESL and EFL students.

作者	Michael A. Putlack & e-Creative Contents
翻譯	鄭玉瑋
編輯	丁宥榆／鄭玉瑋
校對	丁宥暄
製程管理	洪巧玲
發行人	黃朝萍
出版者	寂天文化事業股份有限公司
電話	+886-(0)2-2365-9739
傳真	+886-(0)2-2365-9835
網址	www.icosmos.com.tw
讀者服務	onlineservice@icosmos.com.tw
出版日期	2024 年 1 月　三版再刷（寂天雲隨身聽 APP 版）（0302）

國家圖書館出版品預行編目 (CIP) 資料

FUN 學美國英語閱讀課本：各學科實用課文 (寂天雲隨身聽 APP 版) / Michael A. Putlack, e-Creative Contents 著；丁宥暄，鄭玉瑋譯 . -- 三版 . -- [臺北市]：寂天文化, 2023.01- 印刷
冊；　公分
ISBN 978-626-300-174-9 (第 3 冊：菊 8K 平裝)

1.CST: 英語 2.CST: 讀本

805.18　　　　　　　　111021074

Copyright © 2021 by Key Publications
Photos © Jupiterimages Corporation / Shutterstock
Copyright © 2023 by Cosmos Culture Ltd.
All rights reserved. 版權所有　請勿翻印
郵撥帳號 1998620-0　寂天文化事業股份有限公司
訂書金額未滿 1000 元，請外加運費 100 元。
〔若有破損，請寄回更換，謝謝。〕

FÜN學

美國英語閱讀課本

各學科實用課文 三版

3

Workbook

AMERICAN
SCHOOL
TEXTBOOK

READING KEY

作者 Michael A. Putlack & e-Creative Contents　　譯者 鄭玉瑋

01 How Transportation Has Changed

A Listen to the passage and fill in the blanks. 🎧 37

New _____ changes the way people live.

Technology is using _____ to make things faster or better.

Let's learn how _____ has changed thanks to technology.

In the past, it _____ days to travel by horse and wagon.

Nowadays, people travel faster and _____ in many ways.

We drive cars, _____, and buses.

We ride on trains and _____.

We sail on ships and even fly on _____.

Many kinds of transportation are also used to _____ goods.

A truck can carry _____ all over the country.

A train can carry a lot of goods _____ _____ _____.

An airplane and ship can take goods _____ the world.

Transportation _____ people and goods from one place to another.

Thanks to new technology, transportation is changing _____ and safely.

B Write the meaning of each word or phrase from Word List (main book p.104) in English.

1 技術；科技 _____
2 方式 _____
3 較好的 _____
4 交通工具 _____
5 由於 _____
6 四輪運貨馬車 _____
7 駕駛（汽車等） _____

8 搭乘 _____
9 地鐵 _____
10 載運 _____
11 貨物；商品 _____
12 同時地 _____
13 快速地 _____
14 安全地 _____

02 Inventors and Inventions

A Listen to the passage and fill in the blanks. 🎧 38

Many people like ＿＿＿＿＿＿＿ new things.

We call these people ＿＿＿＿＿＿＿.

And we call the new things they create ＿＿＿＿＿＿＿.

Some inventors have ＿＿＿＿＿＿＿ our world very much.

Some inventions have changed the way people ＿＿＿＿＿＿＿.

This is ＿＿＿＿＿＿＿ true for two men.

They are Thomas ＿＿＿＿＿＿＿ and Alexander Graham Bell.

Thomas Edison was a ＿＿＿＿＿＿＿ inventor.

He worked hard in his ＿＿＿＿＿＿＿ every day.

He invented ＿＿＿＿＿＿＿ ＿＿＿＿＿＿＿ electric things.

These included the ＿＿＿＿＿＿＿ and a motion picture camera.

Edison also invented the ＿＿＿＿＿＿ ＿＿＿＿＿＿＿ we use today.

Thanks to Edison, people could ＿＿＿＿＿＿＿ their own homes.

Alexander Graham Bell was ＿＿＿＿＿＿＿ by sound and how it moved.

So he invented the ＿＿＿＿＿＿＿.

This let people talk to each other through ＿＿＿＿＿＿＿ wires.

Today, ＿＿＿＿＿＿＿ ＿＿＿＿＿＿ people around the world use telephones to talk to

people miles away. And it is all ＿＿＿＿＿＿＿ of Alexander Graham Bell.

B Write the meaning of each word or phrase from Word List in English.

1 發明家　　　＿＿＿＿＿＿＿＿

2 發明；發明物　＿＿＿＿＿＿＿＿

3 溝通　　　　＿＿＿＿＿＿＿＿

4 尤其　　　　＿＿＿＿＿＿＿＿

5 實驗室　　　＿＿＿＿＿＿＿＿

6 發明　　　　＿＿＿＿＿＿＿＿

7 數百的　　　＿＿＿＿＿＿＿＿

8 留聲機　　　＿＿＿＿＿＿＿＿

9 電影攝影機　＿＿＿＿＿＿＿＿

10 燈泡　　　　＿＿＿＿＿＿＿＿

11 照亮　　　　＿＿＿＿＿＿＿＿

12 被……吸引　＿＿＿＿＿＿＿＿

13 電線　　　　＿＿＿＿＿＿＿＿

14 數百萬；無數的　＿＿＿＿＿＿＿＿

03 Choosing Our Leaders

A Listen to the passage and fill in the blanks.

🎧 39

We live in a _____.

So we _____ _____ most of our government leaders.

We vote in _____.

There are many _____ elections.

There are _____, state, and national elections in the U.S.

In these elections, people _____ _____ different offices.

In local elections, people vote for the _____ of a city.

In state elections, people vote for the governor or _____.

And in national elections, people vote for the _____.

So _____ can vote?

Adult citizens have the _____ to vote in elections.

They must be _____ 18 years old by election day.

Each _____ votes one time.

When the voting is finished, each vote is _____.

The person with the most _____ wins the election.

B Write the meaning of each word or phrase from Word List in English.

1	民主國家 _____	8	競選 _____
2	投票 _____	9	官職 _____
3	政府 _____	10	國會議員 _____
4	選舉 _____	11	成人的；成年人的 _____
5	地方的 _____	12	至少 _____
6	州的 _____	13	投票日 _____
7	國家的 _____	14	計算 _____

04 Presidents' Day in February

A Listen to the passage and fill in the blanks.   🎧 40

George _____ was the first president of the United States.

Americans call him "the father of our _____."

Many people call him the _____ American president.

Washington was _____ _____ February 22, 1732.

Even when he was president, Americans _____ his birthday every

year. Soon, it became a national _____.

It was called Washington's _____.

Abraham Lincoln was the _____ president of the United States.

He won the _____ _____ and helped free black slaves.

Lincoln was born on _____ 12, 1809.

After Lincoln died, people wanted to _____ him, too.

Some people _____ the name of Washington's Birthday.

They began _____ it "Presidents' Day."

This let them honor both Washington and _____.

Today, Americans celebrate Presidents' Day on _____ _____ Monday in

February. Schools, banks, and many offices are _____ to show respect for

two great American leaders.

B Write the meaning of each word or phrase from Word List in English.

1 最偉大的   _____
2 出生   _____
3 慶祝   _____
4 生日   _____
5 國定假日   _____
6 贏；獲勝   _____

7 美國內戰；南北戰爭 _____
8 解放   _____
9 奴隸   _____
10 給……以榮譽 _____
11 關閉   _____
12 表示尊敬   _____

05 Countries Have Neighbors

A 💬 **Listen to the passage and fill in the blanks.** 🎧 41

The United States is part of a _____ called North America.

A continent is a very large _____ of land.

In fact, the United States is not _____ country in North America.

It has _____ neighbors.

To the north of the country is _____.

To the south of the country is _____.

Both Canada and Mexico _____ the U.S.

The U.S. has other _____, too.

The _____ is situated to the south of it.

There are many _____ in the sea.

Cuba, _____, and the Dominican Republic are there.

Also, to the north, _____ is beside Alaska.

_____ and its neighbors are on the continent of South America.

Brazil is the largest country in _____.

Argentina, _____, and Columbia are there, too.

All of these countries are _____ neighbors.

B 💬 **Write the meaning of each word or phrase from Word List in English.**

1 大陸；大洲 _____
2 數個的 _____
3 接觸 _____
4 加勒比海 _____
5 位於 _____
6 古巴 _____
7 海地 _____

8 多明尼加共和國 _____
9 俄羅斯 _____
10 巴西 _____
11 南美洲 _____
12 阿根廷 _____
13 智利 _____
14 哥倫比亞 _____

06 The Amazon Rain Forest

A Listen to the passage and fill in the blanks. 🎧 42

The Amazon River is the world's second _____ river.

It is _____ in South America.

It flows mostly in Brazil, but it goes _____ seven other countries, too.

_____ the Amazon River is an enormous rain forest.

It is the Amazon _____.

The Amazon rain forest is the _____ jungle in the world.

Inside it, there is an _____ amount of life.

Around _____ _____ all of the world's animal species live there.

Over 500 _____ of mammals, almost 500 types of reptiles, and huge

numbers of _____ birds live there.

Scientists think around _____ _____ species of insects live there.

There are a wide _____ of trees, plants, and flowers, too.

Today, however, some of the Amazon rain forest is getting _____ _____.

This is making the rain forest smaller, _____ _____ destroying the home

of many plants and animals.

We need to protect the _____.

Without the rain forest, millions of plants and animals _____ _____.

B Write the meaning of each word or phrase from Word List in English.

1 座落於　　　_____
2 流動　　　　_____
3 經過　　　　_____
4 圍繞　　　　_____
5 廣大的　　　_____
6 （熱帶）雨林 _____
7 令人驚訝的；驚人的 _____
8 物種　　　　_____

9 哺乳動物　　_____
10 爬蟲類　　　_____
11 熱帶的　　　_____
12 熱帶鳥類　　_____
13 種類繁多的　_____
14 砍伐　　　　_____
15 破壞　　　　_____
16 保護　　　　_____

07 Protecting the Earth

A Listen to the passage and fill in the blanks. 🎧 43

There are many kinds of _____ _____ on the earth.

We use natural resources _____ _____.

Air, water, _____, plants, and animals are some important resources we use.

Without them, we would not _____ _____ survive.

People have changed the earth in _____ _____.

We cut down trees to build homes and _____.

We make _____ to hold water.

We pave _____ and construct bridges.

We _____ the ground to find fuels such as coal, oil, and gas.

However, we need to be _____ about the changes we make.

Some changes could _____ problems to the earth.

If we cut down too many trees, animals must find new _____ _____ _____.

If they cannot do _____ things, they will die.

When we make _____, we harm natural resources.

If the water and air are not _____, we cannot use them.

Plants and animals could also _____.

We need to use _____ resources and protect more plants and animals.

B Write the meaning of each word or phrase from Word List in English.

1	天然資源	_____	9	建造	_____
2	沒有	_____	10	橋	_____
3	能	_____	11	挖掘地底	_____
4	活下來	_____	12	燃料	_____
5	以許多方式	_____	13	小心仔細的	_____
6	水壩	_____	14	引起	_____
7	保有；容納	_____	15	污染；污染物	_____
8	鋪、築（路等）	_____	16	危害；傷害	_____

A Listen to the passage and fill in the blanks. 🎧44

There are millions of animals _____ _____ the world.

But some kinds of animals are _____.

This means that very few of these animals are _____.

If people do not protect them, they _____ all die.

Today, there are over _____ endangered species.

These animals live in many _____.

The _____ _____, a huge bird, is an endangered animal in the

United States.

The _____ _____ in China is endangered, too.

So is the _____ _____ in India.

Even animals in the _____ are endangered.

The _____ _____ in the Pacific Ocean and the _____ turtle in

the Atlantic Ocean are two of these.

People are _____ ways to protect many endangered animals.

Some endangered animals live in _____ _____ and are being

watched carefully.

The hunting of endangered animals is strictly _____ by laws.

B Write the meaning of each word or phrase from Word List in English.

1 瀕臨絕種的 _____
2 加州兀鷲 _____
3 大熊貓 _____
4 孟加拉虎 _____
5 藍鯨 _____
6 赤蠵龜 _____

7 國家公園 _____
8 看護；注意 _____
9 小心地 _____
10 打獵 _____
11 嚴格地 _____
12 禁止 _____

09 World Religions

A 🔊 Listen to the passage and fill in the blanks. 🎧 45

There are many _____ in the world.

The _____ of most religions believe in a god or gods.

Followers of _____ believe that Jesus Christ is the son of God.

They are called _____.

Christians have a holy book called the _____.

Christians go to _____ on Sunday and on other special days.

Followers of _____ do not believe in any gods.

They are called _____.

Buddhists believe that they _____ to life after they die.

Many Buddhists live in _____.

Followers of _____ believe that Muhammad was a _____ of Allah.

_____ is the name of the Islamic god.

Believers in Islam are called _____.

Followers of _____ believe in one god and in many gods.

For Hindus, the one god is called _____.

But they believe that there are also _____ _____ different gods who
are like different _____ or names of Brahma.

B 💬 Write the meaning of each word or phrase from Word List in English.

1	宗教	_____	11	伊斯蘭教	_____
2	信仰者；信徒	_____	12	穆罕默德	_____
3	信仰	_____	13	先知	_____
4	基督教	_____	14	阿拉	_____
5	耶穌	_____	15	伊斯蘭教的	_____
6	基督教徒	_____	16	信仰者	_____
7	神聖的書；聖典	_____	17	伊斯蘭教徒；穆斯林	_____
8	聖經	_____	18	印度教	_____
9	佛教	_____	19	印度教徒	_____
10	佛教徒	_____	20	梵天	_____

10 Religious Holidays

Every religion has _____.

They are often called _____ _____.

_____ has several holy days.

The two most important days are Christmas and _____.

Christmas is celebrated on _____ 25 every year.

On Christmas, Christians celebrate the _____ of Jesus Christ.

Many Christians go to church and _____ on Christmas.

Easter is the other _____ Christian holy day.

Easter is celebrated in late March or early April _____ _____.

On Easter, Christians celebrate the _____ of Jesus Christ.

They believe that _____ _____ came back to life on Easter.

Islam is another religion with _____ holidays.

One of the most important is _____.

Ramadan _____ for an entire month.

During Ramadan, Muslims must _____ during the day.

So they cannot eat or drink anything _____ the sun is up.

After the sun _____, they can eat.

B Write the meaning of each word or phrase from Word List in English.

1 神聖的 _____
2 幾個的 _____
3 耶誕節 _____
4 復活節 _____
5 十二月 _____
6 （做）禮拜；敬神 _____

7 主要的 _____
8 耶穌復活 _____
9 重生 _____
10 伊斯蘭教齋戒月（九月）_____
11 持續 _____
12 禁食 _____

11 Early Travelers to America

A Listen to the passage and fill in the blanks. 🎧 47

The first people to live in North America were _____ _____.

Many years later, _____ came from Europe.

One early explorer was Christopher _____.

In 1492, he sailed from Spain to find gold and other _____.

He was the _____ of three ships, called the *Pinta*, *Niña*, and *Santa María*.

It was a long _____, but he finally found land.

He was _____ _____ India, but he never got there.

Instead, he _____ the New World: North and South America.

After Columbus, many _____ began sailing to the Americas.

They came from many _____.

They sailed from Spain, Portugal, France, _____, and the Netherlands.

John Cabot of _____ was one explorer.

He _____ around Canada.

Many _____ sailed to the New World.

They _____ Vasco de Balboa, Ponce de León, and Hernando Cortés.

Every year, more and more men came to the _____ _____.

B Write the meaning of each word or phrase from Word List in English.

1	美國原住民	_____	10	新大陸 _____
2	探險家	_____	11	歐洲人 _____
3	航行	_____	12	葡萄牙 _____
4	財富	_____	13	法國 _____
5	船長	_____	14	英國 _____
6	航程	_____	15	荷蘭 _____
7	尋找	_____	16	英格蘭 _____
8	作為替代	_____	17	西班牙人 _____
9	發現	_____	18	包括 _____

12 The Pilgrims and Thanksgiving

A Listen to the passage and fill in the blanks. 🎧48

The Pilgrims were a ＿＿＿＿＿ group of people in England.

They ＿＿＿＿＿ with the Church of England.

They wanted to worship God in their ＿＿＿＿＿ ＿＿＿＿＿.

So, they decided to leave England to look for religious ＿＿＿＿＿.

In ＿＿＿＿＿, the Pilgrims left England to come to America.

They sailed on a ship called the ＿＿＿＿＿.

They ＿＿＿＿＿ ＿＿＿＿ an area of America called Massachusetts.

The Pilgrims built a ＿＿＿＿＿ there called Plymouth.

Their first winter was very ＿＿＿＿＿. 40 people ＿＿＿＿＿ that winter.

The ＿＿＿＿＿ did not know how to live in their new home.

But Wampanoag ＿＿＿＿＿ saved them.

They showed the Pilgrims how to fish, hunt, and ＿＿＿＿＿ ＿＿＿＿＿.

By fall, the Pilgrims had lots of food and a ＿＿＿＿＿ settlement in America.

The Pilgrims ＿＿＿＿＿ the Native Americans to a meal.

They ＿＿＿＿＿ God for all of the good things they had.

It was the first ＿＿＿＿＿.

B Write the meaning of each word or phrase from Word List in English.

1 清教徒 ＿＿＿＿＿
2 宗教的；篤信宗教的 ＿＿＿＿＿
3 不同意…… ＿＿＿＿＿
4 以自己的方式 ＿＿＿＿＿
5 英國國教 ＿＿＿＿＿
6 五月花號 ＿＿＿＿＿
7 登陸 ＿＿＿＿＿
8 殖民地 ＿＿＿＿＿
9 如何…… ＿＿＿＿＿
10 美國萬帕諾亞印第安人 ＿＿＿＿＿
11 種植 ＿＿＿＿＿
12 挽救 ＿＿＿＿＿
13 成功的 ＿＿＿＿＿
14 邀請 ＿＿＿＿＿
15 感謝 ＿＿＿＿＿
16 感恩節 ＿＿＿＿＿

13 Inside the Earth

A Listen to the passage and fill in the blanks. ∩ 49

We live on the _____ surface.

However, _____ us, the earth has several different layers.

They are the _____, mantle, and core.

The crust is the thin _____ layer of the earth.

That's the _____ of the earth that we live on.

All of the earth's water and land—mountains, rivers, oceans, and continents—

_____ _____ the earth's crust.

The mantle is the _____ _____ below the crust.

It is the earth's _____ layer and is full of hot melted rock.

In fact, the _____ is very hot.

The deeper the mantle, the _____ it gets.

At the center of the earth is the _____.

There are two parts: the outer core and the _____ _____.

The outer core is _____ hot and is mostly liquid metal.

The inner core is _____ solid iron and nickel.

B Write the meaning of each word or phrase from Word List in English.

1	地球表面	_____	10	熔化的	_____
2	在……之下	_____	11	熔岩	_____
3	地層	_____	12	較深的	_____
4	地殼	_____	13	地核外核	_____
5	地函	_____	14	極端地；非常	_____
6	地核	_____	15	液體	_____
7	最外部的	_____	16	地核內核	_____
8	組成	_____	17	固體的	_____
9	最厚的	_____	18	鎳	_____

Daily Test

14 Earthquakes and Volcanoes

A Listen to the passage and fill in the blanks. 🎧 50

Sometimes, the ground begins _____.

This shaking can last for a few _____ or several minutes.

This is an _____.

Earthquakes happen when parts of the crust move _____.

Most earthquakes are not powerful, but some are very _____.

They can _____ roads and destroy buildings.

Earthquakes can also _____ the earth's surface.

They can cause the land to _____ or rise.

In some places, hot melted rock _____ out of the ground.

This is a _____.

The hot melted rock, called _____, comes from the mantle.

When a volcano _____, ash, gases, and magma flow onto the earth's surface.

Magma is called lava when it _____ the earth's surface.

_____ can destroy anything that it touches. But it can also _____.

When volcanoes in the water erupt, the lava that comes out often _____ and makes islands.

The _____ _____ were formed this way by volcanoes.

B Write the meaning of each word or phrase from Word List in English.

1	搖晃;震動	_____	9	岩漿	_____
2	地震	_____	10	爆發	_____
3	強大的	_____	11	灰塵;灰燼	_____
4	強烈的	_____	12	熔岩	_____
5	爆裂	_____	13	到達	_____
6	下沉	_____	14	冷卻	_____
7	爆炸	_____	15	夏威夷群島	_____
8	火山	_____	16	形成	_____

15 Why Does the Moon Seem to Change?

A Listen to the passage and fill in the blanks. 🎧 51

The largest object in the _____ _____ is the moon.

But the moon's _____ seems to change every day.

Sometimes we can see all or _____ _____ it.

Sometimes we cannot see it _____ _____.

In fact, the moon does not change its _____.

The moon is a huge _____ _____ _____ that moves around Earth.

The moon does not make its own light _____ stars do.

It looks bright because it _____ light from the sun.

As the moon _____ Earth, the lit part of the moon that we can see changes each night.

This is why the moon _____ _____ change shape.

The different moon shapes are called the _____ _____ the moon.

The four main phases of the moon are new moon, _____ _____, full moon, and last quarter.

It takes about _____ _____ for the moon to go through all of its phases.

B Write the meaning of each word or phrase from Word List in English.

1 物體 _____
2 外觀 _____
3 似乎 _____
4 球（體） _____
5 圍繞……運行 _____
6 如同（口語用法）_____
7 反射 _____

8 繞……軌道運行 _____
9 明亮的；被照亮的 _____
10 【天】相 _____
11 新月 _____
12 上弦月 _____
13 滿月 _____
14 下弦月 _____

Daily Test 16 The First Man on the Moon

A Listen to the passage and fill in the blanks. 🎧 52

On October 4, 1957, the Soviet Union sent a _____ into outer space.
This began the _____ _____ between the Soviet Union and the
United States.

Then, in 1961, President John F. Kennedy made a _____.
He _____ that America would send a man to the moon before the 1960s
ended.
The American _____ _____ began sending many men into space
after that.

Finally, in 1969, the United States was _____ _____ visit the moon.
On July 16, _____ ____ was launched from the Kennedy Space Center.
It was the third _____ _____ of NASA's Apollo Program.
Four days later, on July 20, the *Apollo 11* mission landed the first _____
on the moon.
Neil Armstrong and Buzz Aldrin became _____ _____ humans to walk on
the moon.
Astronaut Michael Collins _____ _____ orbit around the moon.
On July 24, all three men _____ home safely.

B Write the meaning of each word or phrase from Word List in English.

1 蘇聯 _____
2 衛星 _____
3 外太空 _____
4 太空競賽 _____
5 宣告 _____
6 宣布 _____
7 太空計畫 _____
8 阿波羅 11 號 _____
9 發射 _____
10 甘迺迪太空總署 _____
11 月亮的 _____
12 登月計畫 _____
13 太空人 _____
14 運行軌道 _____

17 Electricity

A Listen to the passage and fill in the blanks. ∩ 53

Electricity is a form of _____.

It _____ power for many things to work.

Thanks to electricity, light bulbs _____, and radios play music.

Telephones use _____ to carry sound.

You need electricity to run your _____ and TV.

Without electricity, many things we use every day _____ _____ work.

An _____ runs through a wire.

_____ carry electricity into your home and school.

Electricity moves from outlets, through _____ and wires, into electric machines.

When you turn on a light at home, you are letting electricity _____

_____ wires to the light bulb.

You can also get electricity from _____.

A _____ needs electricity to work.

But you don't need to plug it into _____.

Instead, you just put batteries _____ _____.

A battery can _____ energy inside it and change the energy into electricity.

B Write the meaning of each word or phrase from Word List in English.

1	電	_____	8	通過	_____
2	能量	_____	9	電線	_____
3	提供	_____	10	電源插座	_____
4	電力	_____	11	插頭	_____
5	發亮	_____	12	打開	_____
6	啟動；傳送	_____	13	電池	_____
7	電流	_____	14	手電筒	_____

18 Conserving Electricity

A Listen to the passage and fill in the blanks. 🎧 54

Refrigerators, TVs, computers, and _____ all use electricity.

So do many other _____ that we commonly use.

Why is it important to _____ electricity?

We use _____ _____, such as coal, oil, and gas, to make electricity.

The supply of fossil fuels is _____.

Once they are gone, they are gone _____.

So we need to _____ them.

This will make the earth's _____ _____ fossil fuels last longer.

It will decrease _____ _____ as well.

How can we save _____?

There are _____ _____ to do this.

We can _____ _____ the lights, computers, and TVs when we are not using them.

We should not keep refrigerators open _____ ___ _____ _____.

In the summer, use your _____ _____ less often.

In the winter, don't turn _____ _____ up too high.

Take buses and trains or _____ _____ _____ when you can.

B Write the meaning of each word or phrase from Word List in English.

1	冰箱	_____	9	節省	_____
2	電器；設備	_____	10	減少	_____
3	通常地	_____	11	污染	_____
4	節省	_____	12	空氣污染	_____
5	化石燃料	_____	13	關掉	_____
6	供應	_____	14	冷氣	_____
7	限制；限定	_____	15	暖氣	_____
8	永遠	_____	16	騎腳踏車	_____

Daily Test 19 Motion and Forces

A Listen to the passage and fill in the blanks. ∩ 55

There are many ways _____ move.

Things can move forward and _____, curve, or zigzag.

When something is moving, it is _____ _____.

Different _____ move at different speeds.

Speed is how fast something moves over a _____ _____.

_____ move at very slow speeds.

Airplanes move at very high _____.

Many things can move with _____ _____ force.

A force is _____ _____ _____ _____ _____ that makes an object move.

_____ can change an object's motion and speed.

Gravity is one of _____ forces.

Gravity is the force that pulls things _____ _____.

Things fall to the ground because they are pulled by Earth's _____.

Friction occurs when two objects _____ _____ each other.

_____ can slow down or stop objects in motion.

Bike _____ use friction to stop the bike.

B Write the meaning of each word or phrase from Word List in English.

1	向前	_____	9	距離	_____
2	向後	_____	10	蝸牛	_____
3	彎曲;以曲線行進	_____	11	力	_____
4	成 Z 字形;以 Z 字形進行	_____	12	地心引力	_____
5	運動;移動	_____	13	朝向	_____
6	運動中;移動中	_____	14	摩擦力	_____
7	速度	_____	15	摩擦	_____
8	某種(或一定)程度的	_____	16	煞車	_____

20 Magnets

A · **Listen to the passage and fill in the blanks.** 🎧 56

Magnets _____ things toward them.

Put some _____ _____, rubber bands, or pens on a table.

Bring a _____ near them. Which _____ will the magnet pull?

Magnets _____, or pull, things made of iron or steel.

But magnets do not attract things made of plastic, paper, or _____.

Magnets can also _____ or pull other magnets.

All magnets have two _____.

The N shows the _____ _____.

The S shows the _____ _____.

_____ poles attract each other.

If the N pole of one magnet is _____ the S pole of another magnet, the poles attract each other.

Like poles _____ each other.

If you bring two N poles or two S poles together, they will repel one another.

We use magnets _____ _____ _____.

One of the most _____ _____ is a compass.

A _____ compass needle can show us which direction we are going.

There are magnets in _____ _____ and televisions.

_____ _____ and bank cards also have magnets.

B · **Write the meaning of each word or phrase from Word List in English.**

1	磁鐵	_____	9	磁極	_____
2	迴紋針	_____	10	北極	_____
3	橡皮筋	_____	11	南極	_____
4	帶來；拿來	_____	12	相對的	_____
5	吸引	_____	13	排斥	_____
6	鐵	_____	14	有磁性的	_____
7	鋼	_____	15	羅盤的指針	_____
8	塑膠	_____	16	信用卡	_____

21 What Is Sound?

Listen to the passage and fill in the blanks. 🎧 57

Sound is a form of energy that is made by _____.

To make sound, you need to make _____ move.

When you hit a drum, it _____ and makes sound.

You hear a _____ _____ because a small speaker inside it vibrates.

All objects _____ _____ when they vibrate.

_____ the vibrations stop, the sounds stop.

Sound _____ through the air.

When something vibrates, _____ _____ around it vibrates, too.

Then, it produces _____ _____.

You hear the sound when the sound waves _____ your ear.

Sounds can be loud or soft and high or low, but they are all _____ _____

sound waves.

Sound moves very _____.

It can move _____ meters per second.

We call this the _____ _____ _____.

_____, many airplanes can fly faster than the speed of sound.

Write the meaning of each word or phrase from Word List in English.

1 類型；種類	_____	7 揚聲器	_____
2 由……產生	_____	8 聲波	_____
3 振動	_____	9 大聲的	_____
4 製造聲音	_____	10 每	_____
5 振動	_____	11 每秒鐘	_____
6 電話	_____	12 聲速；音速	_____

22 Sounds and Safety

A Listen to the passage and fill in the blanks. 🎧 58

There are different _____ _____ sounds.

Sounds can be loud or soft and high or _____.

A _____ makes a loud sound. A _____ is soft.

The _____ of a sound is how loud or soft it is.

A _____ makes a sound with a high pitch.

The _____ of a sound is how high or low it is.

Many people _____ very loud sounds.

Some _____ loud sounds can even hurt people's ears.

But not all loud sounds are _____.

Some sounds warn you about _____.

In fact, some loud sounds can save people's _____.

_____ _____ can produce very loud sounds.

They tell you to move to a _____ _____.

Smoke _____ are similar to fire alarms.

When there is smoke, they make loud _____.

_____ and police cars have loud sirens and flashing lights.

They warn other drivers on the road of an _____.

B Write the meaning of each word or phrase from Word List in English.

1 警報器 _____
2 低語；耳語；悄悄話 _____
3 音量；響度 _____
4 口哨；哨音 _____
5 音高 _____
6 不喜歡 _____
7 極端地；非常 _____
8 傷害 _____
9 警告 _____
10 危險 _____
11 挽救 _____
12 生命 _____
13 火災警示器 _____
14 煙霧探測器 _____
15 救護車 _____
16 緊急情況 _____

A Listen to the passage and fill in the blanks. ⌒59

There are many different _____ in your body.

Every organ has its own _____ function.

They also work together as _____ _____ the organ systems.

Some of the most important organs are the _____, brain, and lungs.

The heart is part of the _____ system.

It _____ blood all throughout the body.

The brain runs the body's _____ system.

It sends _____ all around your body.

It controls both _____ and physical activities.

The lungs are part of the _____ system.

They _____ you to breathe.

The stomach, liver, and _____ help the body digest food.

The _____ breaks food into small pieces.

The liver produces _____ and sends them to the small intestine to help it further digest food.

The _____ also cleans your blood.

The large and small intestines absorb _____ from food.

B Write the meaning of each word or phrase from Word List in English.

1	器官	12	訊息
2	獨一無二的	13	控制
3	功能	14	精神上的
4	心臟	15	身體上的
5	腦	16	呼吸的
6	肺	17	呼吸系統
7	循環的	18	胃
8	血液循環系統	19	肝
9	一抽一吸；以幫浦方式輸送	20	腸
10	神經的	21	消化
11	神經系統	22	化學物質

24 The Five Senses

A Listen to the passage and fill in the blanks. 🎧 60

You have five _____ that help you react to your surroundings.

They are sight, smell, hearing, taste, and _____.

The eyes, nose, ears, _____, and skin are the sense organs in your body.

You use your _____ to see with.

The _____ _____ help you see things.

Thanks to _____, you can read books, watch movies, and do other activities.

You use your _____ to smell with.

There are all kinds of _____.

Some are _____ while others are not so nice.

Your ears _____ you hear the things around you.

Sounds travel through the air _____ _____.

When some of those sound waves enter your ears and make your _____ vibrate, you hear the sound.

Your tongue helps you _____ things you eat and drink.

Sweet, sour, _____, and salty are the main four tastes.

Your skin _____ you your sense of touch.

You can feel things _____, especially through your sense of touch.

B Write the meaning of each word or phrase from Word List in English.

1 感官	_____	10 感覺器官	_____
2 五大感官	_____	11 視神經	_____
3 反應	_____	12 令人舒服（愉快）的	_____
4 視覺	_____	13 鼓膜；耳膜	_____
5 嗅覺	_____	14 甜的	_____
6 聽覺	_____	15 酸的	_____
7 味覺	_____	16 苦的	_____
8 觸覺	_____	17 鹹的	_____
9 舌頭	_____	18 身體上地	_____

25 Word Problems

A Listen to the passage and fill in the blanks. 🎧 61

As you practice math, you will do many _____ _____.

When you solve a word problem, you need to _____ what the word problem is asking you to do.

What is this word problem _____ you to do?

There are five _____ on a leaf. Soon, seven more beetles _____ them. How many beetles are there _____ _____?

This is an _____ problem.

To solve it, you can write a _____ _____ like this: 5＋7＝12.

Number sentences _____ words with numbers.

The numbers you add, 5 and 7, are called the _____.

The answer you get, 12, is called the _____.

Now try _____ word problem.

Kevin brings ten cookies to the _____. He _____ four of them.

How many _____ are left now?

This is a _____ problem.

To solve it, you can write a number sentence _____ _____: 10－4＝6.

The number left over, 6, is called the _____.

The signs in a number sentence, such as ＋ *(plus)*, － *(minus)*, and ＝ *(equals)*, are called the _____.

B Write the meaning of each word or phrase from Word List in English.

1 應用題 _____
2 解答 _____
3 瞭解；明白；計算出 _____
4 甲蟲 _____
5 加法題 _____
6 算式 _____
7 取代 _____

8 加數 _____
9 和 _____
10 野餐 _____
11 減法題 _____
12 剩餘（下）的 _____
13 差 _____
14 運算符號 _____

26 Place Value

A Listen to the passage and fill in the blanks. 🎧 62

In math, there are ten _____.

They are 0, 1, 2, 3, 4, 5, 6, 7, 8, and _____.

Each digit has a certain _____.

A number from 0 to 9 is a _____ number.

But we can put two digits together to make a _____ number.

For _____, 10 is a number with two digits.

A two-digit number has a value from 10 to _____.

A _____ number has three digits together.

For example, _____ is a number with three digits.

A three-digit number has a value from 100 to _____.

We know the value of each digit because of _____ _____.

The value of each number is _____ by its location.

Look at the number _____.

The 2 is in the _____ _____, so its value is 200.

The 4 is in the _____ _____, so its value is 40.

The 5 is in the _____ _____, so its value is 5.

In other words, 245 means that it has 2 hundreds, 4 _____, and 5 _____.

B Write the meaning of each word or phrase from Word List in English.

1 數字 _____

2 數值 _____

3 一位數的;個位數的 _____

4 放在一起 _____

5 兩位數的 _____

6 三位數的 _____

7 位值 _____

8 決定 _____

9 位置 _____

10 百位數 _____

11 十位數 _____

12 個位數 _____

A Listen to the passage and fill in the blanks. 🎧 63

Imagine you have 5 _____ of oranges with 3 oranges each.

How many _____ do you have?

You could add them _____ like this: 3+3+3+3+3= _____.

Or, you could use _____. 5×3=15.

When you multiply, you add equal groups of numbers _____ _____.

It is a _____ _____ of adding the same number over and over again.

When you multiply, the numbers that are being _____ are the factors.

And the answer is the _____.

Now, imagine you have _____ apples.

You want to make them 4 groups with _____ _____ number of apples.

You can find the answer by using _____. 20÷4=5.

You can make 4 groups that have _____ apples each.

Division separates a number into _____ _____.

The _____ is the big number being divided.

The divisor is the number doing the _____.

And the _____ is the answer.

B Write the meaning of each word or phrase from Word List in English.

1	想像	_____	8	（乘）積 _____
2	乘法	_____	9	除法 _____
3	做乘法；相乘	_____	10	分開 _____
4	等量	_____	11	被除數 _____
5	多次	_____	12	除以 _____
6	快速的	_____	13	除數 _____
7	因數	_____	14	商 _____

A Listen to the passage and fill in the blanks. 🎧 64

Sometimes, we want to count _____.

Counting _____ _____ _____ can be very slow.

But, if we _____ _____, we can count much faster.

Let's count to _____: 1, 2, 3, 4, 5, 6, 7, 8, 9, 10.

Now let's skip count to ten _____ _____: 2, 4, 6, 8, 10.

Skip counting by twos was _____ _____ faster than using every number.

Now, let's skip count _____ _____: 5, 10, 15, 20, 25, 30, 35, 40, 45, 50.

And let's skip count _____ _____: 10, 20, 30, 40, 50, 60, 70, 80, 90, 100.

Every time we skip count, we can _____ other numbers.

This _____ us count to big numbers very quickly.

We can even skip count _____.

Skip count backward by twos: 10, 8, 6, 4, 2, _____.

What's the _____ way to learn skip counting?

It is to learn the multiplication _____.

They _____ you how to skip count by many different numbers.

B Write the meaning of each word or phrase from Word List in English.

1 一個一個地 _____

2 跳數 _____

3 以 2 的倍數 _____

4 兩倍 _____

5 以 5 的倍數 _____

6 以 10 的倍數 _____

7 省略 _____

8 反向地；向後 _____

9 最簡單的 _____

10 九九乘法表 _____

29 What Are Myths?

A Listen to the passage and fill in the blanks. 🎧 65

Myths are stories that have been around for _____ years or more.

A long time ago, people thought the world was very _____.

They did not understand many of the things they saw and _____.

So they often _____ _____ stories.

These stories _____ the world they lived in.

Today, we call these stories _____.

People all _____ the world have myths.

Many myths are _____.

They often have gods and _____ in them.

Some myths are stories about brave _____ and terrible monsters.

Some myths explain things like how the world began, why we have different

seasons, or what _____ to people after they die.

Although we do not believe these stories, we still enjoy them because they are

so _____.

Some of the most famous myths come to us from _____ Greece and

Rome. We call them Greek and Roman _____.

B Write the meaning of each word or phrase from Word List in English.

1 神話   _____
2 神秘的   _____
3 經驗   _____
4 杜撰   _____
5 相似的   _____
6 女神   _____
7 勇敢的   _____
8 英雄   _____
9 可怕的   _____
10 怪物   _____
11 雖然   _____
12 古代的   _____
13 希臘神話   _____
14 羅馬神話   _____

Daily Test 30 Prometheus Brings Fire

A Listen to the passage and fill in the blanks. 🎧 66

Here is a Greek myth about how _____ got fire.

Once, only giant _____ and gods lived on the earth.

_____ was one of the Titans.

One day, _____, the king of the gods, spoke with Prometheus and his

brother Epimetheus.

Zeus ordered them to make some new _____.

Epimetheus made many _____.

He gave these animals some _____.

Prometheus made only one creature: _____.

It _____ him a long time to make man.

So there were no gifts _____ for men.

On the earth, the humans had no _____ and were very cold.

Prometheus _____ _____ for the humans.

He _____ fire from the gods and took it to the people on the earth.

When Zeus found out what Prometheus had done, he was _____.

To punish him, Zeus _____ him to a big rock.

Every day, an eagle _____ _____ and ate his liver.

Years later, Prometheus was finally _____ _____ by Heracles, a great hero.

B Write the meaning of each word or phrase from Word List in English.

1 巨大的　　　_____
2 【希神】泰坦　_____
3 命令　　　　_____
4 生物；動物　_____
5 人類　　　　_____
6 留下　　　　_____

7 對……感到抱歉、覺得可憐 _____
8 狂怒的　　　_____
9 懲罰　　　　_____
10 用鎖鏈綁住　_____
11 飛下　　　　_____
12 釋放　　　　_____

31 Nouns

A Listen to the passage and fill in the blanks. 🎧 67

A noun is a part of speech like a verb or an _____.

A noun _____ a person, place, or thing.

John, *city*, and *book* are all _____.

All nouns are _____ or proper nouns.

A common noun names any _____, place, or thing.

Girl, *school*, and _____ are common nouns.

A proper noun names a _____ person, place, or thing.

Julie, *Mount Everest*, and *Central Elementary School* are _____ _____.

Proper nouns begin with _____ _____.

And we use _____ _____ for common nouns.

All nouns are _____ singular or plural.

A _____ noun means there is just one of it.

A _____ noun means there are two or more of it.

We often make plural nouns by _____ -s, -es, or -ies to singular nouns.

Boy, *watch*, and _____ are singular nouns.

Boys, _____, and *stories* are plural nouns.

B Write the meaning of each word or phrase from Word List in English.

1	名詞	_____	9	聖母峰	_____
2	詞性	_____	10	小學	_____
3	動詞	_____	11	大寫字母	_____
4	形容詞	_____	12	小寫字母	_____
5	指稱；陳說	_____	13	單數的	_____
6	普通名詞	_____	14	複數的	_____
7	專有名詞	_____	15	單數名詞	_____
8	特定的	_____	16	複數名詞	_____

32 Some Common Sayings

A Listen to the passage and fill in the blanks. 🎧68

Every culture has common _____ or proverbs.

Common sayings or _____ often have special meanings.

They _____ _____ moral messages.

Or they have some _____ that people can learn from.

Many sayings or proverbs are _____ _____ from the oral tradition.

English has many _____ sayings.

"There's no place like home" is a _____ saying.

People use this saying to mean that _____ may be pleasant, but home is the _____ _____ of all.

"Rome wasn't built in a day" is another _____ saying.

This saying _____ us to be patient.

We cannot do _____ things quickly.

So we should take our time and be _____.

"Practice _____ perfect" is a common saying, too.

This saying tells us to _____ trying.

When we try something new, we are usually not _____ _____ it.

But, by _____, we can become perfect at it.

B Write the meaning of each word or phrase from Word List in English.

1	普通的；常見的	_____	9	一天中
2	俗諺	_____	10	熟悉的
3	諺語	_____	11	勸告
4	道德的	_____	12	耐心的
5	智慧	_____	13	練習
6	流傳下來	_____	14	精通的
7	口述傳統	_____	15	保持；繼續不斷
8	眾所皆知的；知名的	_____	16	擅長

33 Realistic Art and Abstract Art

A Listen to the passage and fill in the blanks. ∩ 69

Artists paint many kinds of _____.

But we can divide all art into two _____ groups: realistic art and abstract art.

_____ _____ shows objects as they look in reality.

In realistic art, the landscape would look _____ like it does in reality.

So the trees, mountains, and rivers would look _____.

Rembrandt, a Dutch artist, was a famous realistic _____.

_____ _____ shows objects different from how they look in reality.

Abstract paintings create _____ in new and unusual ways.

For example, abstract landscapes would not look exactly as they do

_____ _____.

The trees _____ _____ green balls.

The mountains might be _____ _____.

And the rivers might be _____ _____.

They would not look like real trees, _____, and rivers at all.

B Write the meaning of each word or phrase from Word List in English.

1 藝術家；畫家 _____
2 繪畫 _____
3 圖畫 _____
4 （劃）分 _____
5 分開的 _____
6 寫實的 _____
7 寫實藝術 _____
8 抽象的 _____
9 抽象藝術 _____
10 真實 _____
11 精確地 _____
12 真實的；現實的 _____

34 Picasso and His Work

A Listen to the passage and fill in the blanks.　🎧70

There have been many _____ artists.

One of the _____ was Pablo Picasso.

Picasso was a Spaniard who painted during the _____ century.

Picasso used many different _____ in his paintings.

One of his most famous styles was _____.

He painted objects in different _____ shapes.

So he used _____, rectangles, and triangles in his paintings.

Picasso was not just a _____.

He was also a _____ and printmaker.

He even drew many _____.

He was _____ _____ all different kinds of art.

One of his most famous paintings _____ _____ Guernica.

It was a _____ painting.

He made it to show his _____ feelings.

During his life, Picasso made thousands of _____.

Today, people spend millions of _____ buying his paintings and other works.

B Write the meaning of each word or phrase from Word List in English.

1 二十世紀 _____
2 主要地；大部分地 _____
3 繪畫 _____
4 立體主義 _____
5 幾何圖形 _____
6 畫家 _____
7 雕刻家 _____
8 版畫家 _____
9 畫 _____
10 素描 _____
11 反戰的 _____
12 藝術作品 _____

A Listen to the passage and fill in the blanks. 🎧 71

There are many _____ kinds of music.

One of them is _____ music.

Classical music _____ mostly on musical instruments.

The piano, violin, cello, and flute are some _____ classical music instruments.

There are many _____ _____ classical music, too.

A long piece of music played by an orchestra is called a _____.

A _____ is for an orchestra, too.

But it has some parts for _____ to play.

Operas and _____ music are two other forms of music that involve singing.

_____ _____ are songs that have been passed down for many years.

Every country has _____ own folk music.

It is usually fun to _____ _____.

Most _____ music is folk music.

Patriotic music is songs and music like _____ _____.

Patriotic music makes people feel _____ _____ their country.

B Write the meaning of each word or phrase from Word List in English.

1 古典音樂 _____
2 依賴；依靠 _____
3 受歡迎的 _____
4 一段曲子 _____
5 交響樂 _____
6 協奏曲 _____
7 獨奏者 _____
8 歌劇 _____
9 聖歌音樂 _____
10 需要；包含 _____
11 民謠 _____
12 愛國的 _____
13 國歌 _____
14 對……感到驕傲 _____

36 Modern Music

A Listen to the passage and fill in the blanks. 🎧 72

What kind of _____ do you like?

People have different _____ in music.

Some _____ classical music. Others like _____ pop music.

Some _____ _____ sing and play music. Others like _____ _____ music.

Let's _____ _____ more about modern music.

Jazz is a _____ kind of music.

When jazz musicians play, they _____.

They change the words and the _____ while playing, so the music sounds a little different _____ _____.

Different _____ _____ can play the same songs in different ways.

Some people call _____ _____ "rock and roll."

Rock music often _____ guitars and drums.

Most _____ _____ have one or two singers.

Pop music is _____ _____ rock music.

But it often features more _____ music.

It is also like _____ music.

Rap is a _____ new type of music.

Often, rappers speak, not sing, the _____ to their songs.

B Write the meaning of each word or phrase from Word List in English.

1 愛好　　　　　_____

2 現代的　　　　_____

3 流行音樂　　　_____

4 認識　　　　　_____

5 爵士　　　　　_____

6 音樂家　　　　_____

7 即興創作；即興表演　_____

8 歌詞　　　　　_____

9 曲調　　　　　_____

10 搖滾樂　　　　_____

11 以……為特色　_____

12 和……相似　　_____

13 輕快的　　　　_____

14 完全地；簡直　_____

15 饒舌歌手　　　_____

16 歌詞　　　　　_____

MEMO